WHITE CHRISTMAS WEDDING

CELESTE WINTERS

WHITE CHRISTMAS WEDDING

A Novel

HOWARD BOOKS
—
ATRIA

New York   London   Toronto   Sydney   New Delhi

**HOWARD
BOOKS**

ATRIA

An Imprint of Simon & Schuster, Inc.
1230 Avenue of the Americas
New York, NY 10020

First Howard Books/Atria Paperback edition October 2019

HOWARD BOOKS / **ATRIA** PAPERBACK and colophon are trademarks of Simon & Schuster, Inc.

For information about special discounts for bulk purchases, please contact Simon & Schuster Special Sales at 1-866-506-1949 or business@simonandschuster.com.

The Simon & Schuster Speakers Bureau can bring authors to your live event. For more information or to book an event, contact the Simon & Schuster Speakers Bureau at 1-866-248-3049 or visit our website at www.simonspeakers.com.

Manufactured in the United States of America

1   3   5   7   9   10   8   6   4   2

Library of Congress Cataloging-in-Publication Data

Names: Winters, Celeste, author.
Title: White Christmas wedding : a novel / Celeste Winters.
Description: First Howard Books trade paperback edition. | New York : Howard Books, 2019.
Identifiers: LCCN 2019016688 (print) | LCCN 2019018525 (ebook) | ISBN 9781982128784 (ebook) | ISBN 9781982128777 (paperback)
Subjects: LCSH: Weddings—Fiction. | Christmas stories. | BISAC: FICTION / Christian / Romance. | GSAFD: Love stories | Christian fiction.
Classification: LCC PS3623.I67434 (ebook) | LCC PS3623.I67434 W58 2019 (print) | DDC 813/.6—dc23

LC record available at https://lccn.loc.gov/2019016688

ISBN 978-1-9821-2877-7
ISBN 978-1-9821-2878-4 (ebook)

For Joanna and Carolyn, who are gifts all year round

WHITE CHRISTMAS WEDDING

One

"THEY'RE EVEN MORE BEAUTIFUL than I imagined," Jen Fitzgerald said as the florist's assistant set the first box of arrangements down on a folding chair at the end of the nearest row.

And that was saying something. Because Jen had been imagining hosting a wedding in her family's barn for approximately as long as she'd been able to imagine a wedding—so well over twenty years.

It had started with a child's simple logic. Once Jen learned, as a little girl, that all weddings didn't have to happen in a church, because you could just get the minister and take them pretty much anywhere, her five- or six-year-old self hadn't been able to imagine anyplace better to get married than her family's barn. After all, what could be more wonderful than the smell of oats and hay, the dust-mote light pouring through the slits time had opened between the old planks, and the soft noses of her favorite horses?

But as she'd grown up, instead of discarding the idea along with so many of the other silly misconceptions of her childhood, her thoughts of a wedding in the barn had only gotten stronger. When her friends began to pick out hotel ballrooms or rent out the Knights of Columbus hall for their own weddings, Jen always thought back to her own barn and how much more beautiful it would be than a sterile old fluorescent-lit hotel or a dark, low-roofed community club—if it was just done up exactly the right way, by someone who knew how.

And when the craze for barn weddings started up, and she began to see spread after spread of country-themed weddings in the bridal magazines, the idea formed into a plan.

She didn't love her day job, managing the office of Dr. Brown, the town's pediatrician. She liked the kids. She liked Dr. Brown. She liked the small streets of the town, and the friends she'd had all her life, whom she still got together with on weekends, a lot like they had when they were kids. But part of her itched to get out, and see the world—to have a life that had more in it than the confines of Blue Hill, even though there was no other land that was more beloved to her in the world.

And some quick napkin math showed her that if she played her cards right, filling the barn with weddings all summer could give her enough income to do what she wanted for the rest of the year. Her mind began to flood with visions of lace draped from the crossbeams and troughs stuffed with roses—as well as the trips to sunny climates she'd be able to take in the winter: Greece, Argentina, India . . . And then her childhood best friend, Beth Dean, had called from New York City to say she was getting married—and she wanted to do it at home.

The Dean and Fitzgerald farms were neighbors, which in most cases would mean their actual homes were miles apart, but by a quirk of the land they shared, both families' ancestors had built their homes and barns within a stone's throw of one another, probably so both homes could enjoy the vast, gentle rise they both sat upon, which allowed them a commanding view of the fields around them, and even, on clear nights, the twinkling lights of town, miles off. From the property line that divided the two yards, the farms stretched out for acres on either side. And between them was a giant pine tree that the two families had a Christmas tradition of decorating together every year, filling it with lights that could be seen from the hilltop for miles around.

So when Beth had flown back into town months before, trying to figure out how she was possibly going to hold a wedding fancy enough to impress her extremely fancy in-laws-to-be, Jen had mentioned the idea of doing it in the barn where the two of them had spent so many delightful hours together as girls, right there in Blue Hill—and mentioned the fact that she'd be willing to plan the whole thing herself.

Now here she was, although she could barely believe it herself: the night before the very first wedding she'd ever planned.

And the flowers, which she'd been dreaming about for all those years, changing them up from hydrangeas to daisies, from pink orchids to blue iris, from simple clusters of baby's breath to giant swaths of snapdragons and phlox, were prettier than any of the arrangements she had imagined.

They seemed to fill the whole barn, which was saying something, since it was at least the size of a small church, with a peaked roof and a pair of back doors that opened to the fields beyond, almost the same size as the large swinging front doors that Jen had just walked through. On the left was a row of fenced-off areas for storing hay and seed, now cleaned out perfectly and set up as nooks for guests to congregate, or caterers to prepare meals. On the right were stalls that used to hold far more animals than the two horses who now nodded their heads gladly at the far end of the barn, to acknowledge Jen's entrance. Between them was a large expanse of well-scrubbed concrete, now set with all the accoutrements to turn it into a real-live wedding venue, holding a hundred and fifty chairs for the incoming guests.

And at each corner of the barn were four beautiful Christmas trees, set with white lights and wrapped in cream velvet ribbon, with fresh flowers dotted among their branches. Together, they formed a spectacular display of Christmas beauty, and one of the most beautiful floral creations Jen had ever seen.

The florist's assistant was her twelve-year-old daughter, Lindy. Lindy beamed with pleasure at the compliment, and as much pride as Jen thought she'd ever seen.

"Did you help make these?" Jen asked, thinking that must be the reason Lindy looked so proud.

Lindy shook her head, looking down at the sprays of elegant white lilies nestled in fronds of juniper, starred with the tiny blossoms of wax flowers and studded with the bright blue of bachelor buttons, which picked up the fainter blue of the waxy juniper berries, which were also frosted with a faint red. The effect was stunning.

"My mother made them," she said, looking back up.

Jen told herself she should have known. Almost nobody ever looked that proud of themselves. Even in the midst of their biggest accomplishments, most people could always find a way to doubt themselves. The pride she saw in Lindy's eyes was a special kind: the pride a child has in their parent's accomplishments, because only a child knows both everything a parent is capable of—and how hard a parent works to accomplish everything they do.

As Lindy said this, her mom, Pamela, came in, her arms loaded with thick swags of baby's breath, juniper, and thick pale blue velvet ribbon. Jen recognized the look in Pamela's eyes, because she knew the feeling herself: wonder, exhaustion, and a smidge of joy.

This was Pamela's first big gig, as well. She'd been doing prom corsages and holiday centerpieces for her friends for years, and had even worked her way up to doing flowers for a handful of local weddings, where she was famous for turning armfuls of greens cut from the side of the road and flowers collected from the discount bins at the local grocery store into stunning arrangements. But this was the first time she'd worked on a big budget, with hothouse flowers ordered months in advance, rather than whatever she could find in local shops and gardens. She was at least as nervous and thrilled as Jen was, although both of them were working hard not to let on.

"I was just telling Lindy," Jen told her, "these are some of the prettiest flowers I've ever seen."

Pamela, still on task, didn't seem to be able to stop to take the compliment in. "I just want to get them in before they all freeze," she said with a quick grin.

Jen squinted as she looked out the barn door at the sparkling snow that blanketed the surrounding land. Beth and Tom had wanted a Christmas wedding, because they'd first met at a Christmas party, and because Beth had always loved the holiday. And this year, the timing was perfect: Christmas Eve was on a Monday, so almost everyone had the weekend before off, and could take the time to join them for the weekend and still travel home to their families in time for the holiday, just like the old songs sang about. So Beth and Tom had decided it was meant to be—a once-in-a-lifetime chance, not to be missed, to merge their wedding with all the tradition and feeling and sheer beauty of Christmas.

The one thing Jen hadn't been able to guarantee them about their wedding was that it'd be a white one. But the weather of the past weeks had cooperated with Beth's plans, too. The whole town looked like a Christmas card.

When Jen turned back, Pamela had already scampered off,

hanging the juniper swags over the beautiful white metal arch that would be the focal point of the whole ceremony, while Lindy began to carefully remove centerpieces from their travel boxes and set them out on the dinner tables that guests would migrate to after the ceremony, when the rows of ceremony chairs would be cleared to create a dance floor.

Every arrangement that emerged from the box was like a tiny new burst of stars, turning the barn into a whole new constellation.

Jen leaned back against the familiar wood of the barn, letting herself feel her satisfaction—and exhaustion—for one delicious moment. It was barely after noon, and the barn would be fully decorated before she knew it. A few minutes more, and everything would be perfect.

Inside her purse, her phone rang.

As she fumbled for it, Jen felt a ping of anxiety—but not about the details of the wedding. Beth's brother, Jared, was coming home for the wedding. It would be the first time Jen had seen him in years. And before he left, they'd been an inseparable couple for years before that.

She and Ed, whom she'd been seeing since the spring, were happy now. Unlike Jared, Ed didn't have any burning desire to get out of town and see the world. He thought Blue Hill was pretty special, just the way it was, just like her. And also unlike Jared, he was infinitely interested in their relationship. She didn't think Jared even had any idea when the two of them had first started dating. But Ed had asked her out for the first time on the first of June, and on the first of every other month, he always managed to show up with some little trinket or a small bouquet, to celebrate what he liked to call their "anniversary."

So it was driving Jen more than a little nuts that every time her phone rang, she wondered if it was Jared. Not that he'd call her on purpose. But she was the contact number for the entire guest list—anyone who had a question, or a problem. If he needed any little thing during the course of the wedding, there was a good chance she'd have to talk to him. And she didn't know if she was looking forward to that or not.

To her relief, the caller ID came up as Bailey Chester, the local college kid whom she'd hired to drive the charming antique fire truck that she'd hired to serve as a private shuttle for the New Yorkers who were coming from the airport. It was impossible to miss—and it was exactly the kind of country charm that you couldn't get for any price in the city.

"Bailey," she said, her heart warming as she answered the phone. Bailey had been relentlessly conscientious the entire time they'd been working together, always letting her know how things were going at any given moment, to an almost aggravating degree. But she had to admit now that it calmed her nerves to know she was never going to have to struggle to get in touch with him—like it or not, he'd be in touch with her. "How's it going?"

"I'm on I-94," Bailey said.

The noise in the old truck, she noticed, was incredibly loud. It sounded as if the traffic were practically inside with Bailey. But at his news, she smiled. I-94 was exactly where he should be right now, about half an hour out from arriving at the airport, where everyone would land in the next few hours.

"That's great!" Jen said. "Thank you so much, Bailey."

"Wait," Bailey said.

"Yes?" Jen asked.

"I'm on the side of the road," Bailey told her.

"Are you all right?" Jen asked, her face suddenly hot and her hands suddenly cold. "Did something happen?"

"I'm all right," Bailey said. "And so is the truck. Except for the fact that it won't move."

Jen's panicked look took in all the beautiful elements in the barn: the velvet-padded white folding chairs, the thick old wood of the beams, and the garden Pamela was calling forth seemingly out of nothing, even though it was the middle of winter.

Then her mind began to calculate with the details of every itinerary she had practically memorized in the past few weeks.

With a shock, she realized that every single New York guest was already in the air, all expecting to follow the directions she'd given them about finding the fire truck shuttle when they landed.

And right now, nobody was on the way to meet them.

Two

SYLVIA SIMPSON GLANCED OUT the plane window and sighed.

There wasn't a cloud in the icy blue sky, but tens of thousands of feet below, the earth still looked like it was blanketed in cloud cover because of the thick banks of white snow that stretched in every direction, except in a few places where it ran out in what looked to be muddy fields. From this high up, she could see the borders of where snowstorms had squalled. It looked as if someone had thrown giant handfuls of flour or powdered sugar over a span miles square, but at the edges the margins were blurred, as if the flour or sugar had turned thinner and thinner as it spread out.

The land was also incredibly flat, which came at first as a bit of a novelty, since she was most used to the spiky landscape of the city or the low hills of the surrounding states, now half-obscured by freeways and subdivisions. Or the flash of ocean between the East Coast and Europe, which she crossed on a semiregular basis for anything from parties to her business as an art dealer. But the novelty quickly wore off, and the miles and miles of flat land began to seem like a bore, then a waste, and then, as it dragged on and on, simply nonsensical.

"So much snow," Sylvia commented to the woman sitting next to her. "You'd think there'd at least be mountains."

The woman next to her was in her fifties, probably twenty

years Sylvia's senior. She was dressed in a pair of neat blue jeans and a black-and-red plaid shirt, with her reddish hair pulled back on both sides in a pair of simple silver barrettes. With a steady glance, she took in Sylvia's own black cashmere wrap, black pin-thin jeans, and black boots, then raised her eyebrows.

"Mountains?" she repeated. "In Ohio?"

"With all this snow," Sylvia explained, "at least you could ski."

"I guess so," the woman said, and looked back at the maga-zine in her lap, which appeared to be some kind of catalog, not for clothes or furniture, but for plants: dozens of tulip blossoms on one page, stands of daffodils not just in yellow but in pink and white and red on the next.

"Have you been to Michigan before?" Sylvia asked. The flight was scheduled to land there in less than an hour, and before today nothing in the world could have induced her to set foot there, unless someone had inexplicably moved the Venice Biennale to Detroit.

"Born and raised," the woman said.

"I'm Sylvia," Sylvia told her. "Is Michigan nice?"

"Darla," the woman said, with a quick smile. "I guess that depends on what you think is nice."

"Well," Sylvia said. "They have a good art museum in Detroit."

"Never been there," Darla said.

This fact took Sylvia several seconds to absorb. Then it took her several seconds more to smooth the shock off her face.

Darla looked at her with amusement. "You like art?" she asked.

It was such a strange question that Sylvia was stymied for a moment. One could loathe art, or love it, want it, hate it, be sick-ened by it or transformed by it—but like it? Could you just "like" the Taj Mahal? Did people "like" Beethoven's Eighth? How about

Michelangelo's Pietà, with Jesus languishing dead in Mary's arms, and the grief on Mary's face? Were you supposed to "like" that?

She wound up making a strangled noise in her throat that she hoped Darla would take whatever way Darla might "like" best.

"You been to Michigan before?" Darla asked, with what seemed to Sylvia to be perhaps a trace of amusement.

Sylvia shook her head.

"You've never seen a Great Lake?" Darla asked, her voice incredulous.

It was all Sylvia could do not to roll her eyes. How much different could one lake be from another? "I've seen lakes before," she said.

"Not like this," Darla said. "These lakes are so big, you can float an oceangoing ship on them. But they're the only kind of ships like them, anywhere. Transport steel, grain, all over the Midwest. Canada to Chicago, and back again. But you don't get the big seas on them you get in the ocean. So Great Lakes boats don't have to be stubby like ocean vessels, because they don't take the same kind of punishment in the weather. They're the longest large ships in the world."

"You've been on one?" Sylvia asked.

Darla nodded. "My brother," she said. "He ships all over the lakes."

As Sylvia's eyes widened, Darla's narrowed. "What brings you to Michigan?" she asked.

Sylvia sighed with the same theatrical dread she'd responded to that question with when her friends back home in New York had asked her what she was doing, flying to Michigan two days before Christmas. Midsigh, she realized that her joke might not land quite the same way with someone who was actually from

Michigan. So she broke out in a somewhat awkward but nonetheless bright smile.

"One of my best friends is getting married there," she said. "To one of my oldest ones."

Darla raised her eyebrows. "She from Michigan?"

Sylvia resisted the urge to snark a bit about the assumption that her best friend would naturally be a woman. In point of fact, Beth was. Instead, she just nodded. "Blue Hill," she said, feeling a little uncertain to be saying the name of a place where she'd never been—and had no idea what it was like. "Do you know where that is?"

Darla nodded emphatically. "Oh, sure," she said. "Blue Hill's real nice. Some beautiful Hereford stock come from out that way."

Sylvia had never had much of a poker face, and her eyebrows climbed with surprise at hearing Darla talk like one of the society ladies on the Upper East Side, discussing what families would and wouldn't be invited to the Colonial Club that year. But she'd never heard of the Herefords. "Oh?" she said, playing along until she caught up with the situation.

Darla nodded again, this time leaning in confidentially, as if she was about to drop one of the great secrets of Michigan high society. "Although my father always preferred Guernsey, himself."

From the farthest recesses of Sylvia's memory, the mention of the name Guernsey brought up the image of a milk carton in her mind's eye, just as Darla added, "Not everybody agrees, but he always claimed they gave the best milk."

Cows, Sylvia realized. Darla had been talking to her about the merits of different breeds.

"Have you been there yourself?" Sylvia asked, her natural curiosity drawing her on. "To Blue Hill, I mean?"

Darla shook her head. "It's in the opposite direction from me," she said. "I'll be heading west from the airport. You'll be going back east, into all those farms up along the river.

"But I heard good things about it," she added, in what was clearly an attempt to be comforting. "Some of the best strawberries in the country get grown up along that way."

Somehow, that didn't give Sylvia the comfort Darla seemed to think it should. She was completely unconvinced that the country's best strawberries would be enough to make up for all the city comforts she was leaving behind. And even she knew enough to know that there weren't likely to be fresh Michigan strawberries in the stores if there was snow on the ground.

"Where'd you grow up?" Darla asked.

"New York," Sylvia said. If she'd been in the city, she would have told her Park and Seventy-Third, but she knew that would just be Greek to Darla.

Darla nodded. "And that's where you live now?" she said.

Sylvia nodded, trying hard not too look too proud of herself. But to her surprise, Darla looked at her with something approaching sympathy.

"You never lived anywhere else?" Darla asked.

Sylvia shook her head, and barely managed to keep herself from adding, *Where else would you live?*—which she realized probably wouldn't go over in this context quite the way it did in bars in the city.

"Not even for college?" Darla asked.

Sylvia shook her head again. Some of the best schools in the world were right there in New York, she'd pointed out to everyone who would listen at the time. Why wouldn't she go to one of them? "I went in the city," she said.

"Shoot," Darla said. "I bartended in New Orleans for a year

after I graduated high school. And my son Jeff went up to Alaska the last three years running, to process fish. It don't sound like you've seen much of the country, have you?"

Sylvia opened her mouth to object, then realized she didn't have much to object with. She doubted that Darla would accept Miami, LA, and New Orleans as a representative tour of the United States.

In her hand, her phone buzzed.

"They got phones in New York that work on planes?" Darla said, sounding impressed for the first time.

"I put it on the Wi-Fi," Sylvia said. "Once we got up in the air." She squinted down at her phone's screen.

"Oh, no," she said. "It looks like our fire truck broke down."

"Fire truck?" Darla said, looking at Sylvia as if this wedding might be a whole lot more interesting than she had reckoned.

"I guess?" Sylvia said. "They told us to look for the fire truck when we got out to the curb. I guess it was some kind of antique."

Her mind began to race through the options, none of which she liked. If whoever had planned the wedding thought it was a good idea to pile everyone into some rickety old fire truck when they'd just been on a plane for hours, what in the world would their backup plan be once the old heap broke down?

"What do you think they'll do?" Sylvia asked, her eyes wide.

"I wouldn't worry too much," Darla said dryly. "There's more than one automobile in the state of Michigan."

Three

"THAT'S RIGHT!" DESTINY BARD told her six-year-old daughter with a mixture of wonder and elation as a perfectly formed white ribbon bow emerged from Jessie's small, plump, but surprisingly deft hands.

Suddenly, a whole raft of calculations shifted in Destiny's head.

For some reason, she had allowed the words, "Let me know if there's anything else I can do. Anything at all," to escape from her lips the last time she'd talked with Jen about the final details Jen was still struggling to pull together for Beth's wedding, which seemed to grow in size and complexity every time Destiny talked with either Beth or Jen.

But that wasn't her worst mistake. Her worst mistake was when Jen, after a pause, had breathed, "Do you really mean it?"

That's when Destiny should have said, *I mean it with all my heart. But now that I think about it, I actually have two children under seven, and a job my boss is always forgetting is only supposed to be part-time. She doesn't actually care if I'm there forty hours a week. She just wants me to do forty hours' worth of work, whether I'm there or not. My husband's got a full-time job, but his boss seems to think there are two of him. So he's not a heck of a lot of help around the house right now. The dresses down at the bridal shop were such a horrible mix of ugly and expensive that I decided it would be a good idea to sew my own bridesmaid's dress, even though I haven't sewn anything since home ec in eleventh grade. The wedding's this week, and I'm not done yet. So I'm feeling a little overwhelmed now. It's probably better if I don't take on anything extra right this minute.*

But that wasn't what she'd said.

Maybe because she was just a sucker, or maybe because she could hear the desperation in Jen's voice, and recognized it a bit too well herself, she'd said, "Yes."

And that was how she'd wound up with a dining room table full of white tulle, white ribbon, a minor forest full of faux dusty miller, the silvery leaves made from something like real velvet, to mimic the velvety silver leaves of the real thing. As well as several large boxes of giant white column candles that admittedly smelled better than anything Destiny had ever smelled in her life: a mixture of bergamot, grapefruit, and something else obviously stolen from the borderlands of Eden.

Her job: to cut large rounds of the tulle, wrap it around the column candles, and then fasten the spray of tulle at the top with ribbon and dusty miller.

The first one had looked amazing. But it had taken her half an hour of wrestling with the tulle and ribbon, not to mention the faux dusty miller, which seemed to have a burning desire for freedom, leaping from her hand or slipping through the slick folds of the shiny ribbon at the crucial moment, often enough that her three-year-old, Cody, had already pulled on her pant leg to ask her the meaning of one of the strange words she'd let slip in the process.

At that rate, she calculated, she'd be done approximately several weeks after the wedding was over and all the fancy out-of-town guests had flown home.

If only, she had thought, she had another pair of hands.

That's when she had looked down at Jessie, and begun to plot about the possibility of putting her daughter to work—not long enough to interfere with her elementary school education, just long enough to get these stupid candles out the door.

She already knew Jessie was surprisingly dexterous. She'd strung miles of beads on fishing wire when a craze for beaded bracelets had swept through the local kindergarten, and this year at Christmas, the day hadn't even been over before she'd woven all six pot holders from the pot holder–making kit they'd gotten her.

Still, she hadn't had high expectations when she'd called Jessie over. She was just throwing another option at the problem, the same way she'd ground her way through getting the first candle done, trying everything she could think of until she wound up holding a bunch of tulle in her teeth to finally get the ribbon and dusty miller tied off.

"See this?" Destiny had asked her, pointing at the candle she'd spend the better part of an hour creating. "You want to help me make one?"

"Sure!" Jessie had piped, climbing up on the dining room chair. She'd had to stand on the chair rather than sit, to get the height she needed, but once she'd established the correct angle to tackle the problem, she bit her lip, surveyed the carnage on the dining room table, plucked one of several rounds of tulle and a length of ribbon Destiny had already cut, plunked a column candle down in the middle of it, surrounded the candle with tulle, added a spray of dusty miller at the top, and tied it all up in a neat ribbon that covered the unlit wick with a burst of tulle.

It happened so fast, and so much more quickly than it had taken her, that Destiny could barely believe it. She'd seen both her kids accomplish fearsome acts of destruction in what seemed like the turn of a head or the blink of an eye: Jessie had once yanked down an entire velvet window dressing at the home of Carl's boss in the instant that Destiny had turned her back to pour a cup of punch. And Cody had "decorated" the entire main wall of their living room with turquoise marker in the time it had taken her to spread jam and peanut butter on two slices of bread as his lunchtime sandwich.

But this was the first time she'd seen those same skills seemingly used for good. And it shifted the whole math of her day. If Jessie could help with these candles, then Destiny might be able to get something done on her dress *before* Carl got home, which meant that she wouldn't have to work on it when she was exhausted after the rehearsal dinner, or, God forbid, finish it first thing the next morning, on the day of the actual wedding.

She leaned down to give Jessie a kiss, which caused Jessie to look up at her in surprise.

"What, Mommy?" she asked, looking mildly worried.

"You're just doing a great job, honey," Destiny said.

On her pant leg, she felt a familiar tug.

"Wanna help," Cody said, looking up. "Let me."

Cody was *almost* four, as he kept telling anyone who would listen, although Destiny hadn't quite worked out for herself whether this was simply a matter of pride in his age or if he was angling for everyone in town, from the guy at the post office to the checkout lady at the grocery store, to get him a present.

She didn't have any illusions that he'd be able to accomplish the same kind of feat that Jessie just had. But Cody was a bit of a madman with a pair of safety scissors. In his varied and sometimes shocking career as a young artist, he'd recently left the wall drawings of his youth behind and branched out into a kind of paper sculpture, which involved cutting the figures in coloring books *out* of the books, rather than coloring them in.

But in this new phase, Destiny had observed, he was uncannily able to follow the traced lines with his stubby little scissors.

"Okay," she said. "You want to cut out some circles for Mommy?"

Cody nodded gravely.

"Two down!" Jessie called. When Destiny looked over, Jessie was pushing a second perfectly executed column candle, complete with its tulle-and-ribbon hat, to the side, so she could start another one.

Quickly, Destiny traced a large circle on a piece of tulle and handed it to Cody. "You think you can cut along that line for Mommy?"

Cody didn't even nod. He just grabbed the tulle and went to work, shaving away the squared edges to reveal a virtually perfect circle.

"Good boy!" Destiny yelped.

At the worried look that came into Cody's eyes at the praise, Destiny had a brief moment of wondering why both her children seemed mildly unsettled by her outbursts of positive reinforcement. Was it *really* that unusual? But she didn't have time to take the deep dive into parental guilt she might have under other circumstances. There was still a small army of column candles waiting to be wrapped in tulle.

Five minutes later, she'd sketched a giant pile of circles on squared-off pieces of tulle, and managed to sit down at the end table she'd commandeered as her sewing station, to take another pass at sewing the skirt of her blue velvet dress to the bodice while her progeny worked diligently behind her.

She hadn't thought, when she'd picked the pattern out, that she had any particularly grand ambitions. It was a simple, classy design with a scoop neck and three-quarter-length sleeves, which amounted to fewer than eight total pattern pieces, some even simpler than the circles that Cody was now busy cutting out.

But while the pattern was simple, the fabric was not. The one thing Beth had asked for the dresses was that they all be blue, and all be velvet.

Maybe in New York, Destiny thought, they had shops full of nothing but blue velvet dresses. Maybe even a whole street full of them, all side by side, so you could pick the one you liked best out of the thousands that were crowded together there, on all those racks.

But here in Michigan, her few small yards of velvet were a tricky mix. The back of the fabric was slick, and the front of it, with the nap, got hung up easily on the foot by the needle that held the fabric in place. Fastening the bodice to the skirt was a crucial step, but it should have been simple. With velvet, though, you never knew. And of course, Beth would pick velvet. It was just like her: beautiful, totally out of the ordinary for their small town—and totally impractical.

As Destiny guided the fabric through the machine, she tried to reel her feelings in. She didn't like the feeling of being angry at her friend on the eve of her wedding. She'd seen true bridezillas before, and Beth was hardly one of them.

And, truth be told, she realized as the velvet slid under her hands, it wasn't Beth she was frustrated with. It was herself. She and Beth had had all the same dreams growing up. They were both going to get out of town the first chance they had, go to New York, and live a life nobody in Blue Hill could even imagine.

The problem was, Carl had proposed to her when they were still seniors in high school. And although Destiny and Carl hadn't gotten married until their junior year of college, Beth was the only one who had gone to New York, in the end. And Destiny had always wondered what would have happened if she had gone, too, instead of doing what she did.

When she pulled the garment from the machine and turned it right side out again, it was starting to look like an actual dress. And she had to admit, the color was gorgeous: a full-length drape of deep midnight blue that would fall from her shoulders to the floor.

"Wow, Mommy!" Jessie breathed from behind her. "It's so beautiful!"

With a grin, Destiny turned around.

"Do you think I might get a dress like that?" Jessie asked. "For Christmas?"

Destiny raised her eyebrows. Both her kids had always been thrilled by the run-up to Christmas, dazzled by the lights in town, the cookies suddenly available from all the neighbors, and the promise of presents. But this year, the idea that Santa might bring her *anything she wanted* seemed to have gotten a particularly strong hold on Jessie's mind. For weeks, any time anything caught her fancy, she'd asked if Santa might bring her one, too. If everything Jessie kept adding to her growing list actually wound up under their tree on Christmas morning, Santa would have to buy them a new house, too, to accommodate it all.

Still, Destiny couldn't believe what Jessie had accomplished while she was sewing. The entire table was full of wrapped candles, so many that she was surprised the old wings could hold them up.

And Cody was still happily cutting out big circles of tulle.

"You didn't do so bad yourself, honey," she said. "Thank you so much. You've been a big help!"

Pleased, Jessie grinned and plunked her little elbow on the table to show off. The side of the table that was already straining under the weight of all the candles.

And that's when the whole table, in slow motion like a horror shot from a movie, began ever so slightly to tip.

Startled, Jessie lost her footing and took a few false steps.

Destiny managed to scoop her off before she fell.

But with her daughter in her arms, there was nothing she could do to stop the whole table, and all the candles on it, from tipping over and crashing to the ground.

Four

"IS THAT ALL YOU brought?" Beth's mother asked in surprise as Beth led her in-laws-to-be, Gloria and Ken Allerton, into her mother's kitchen.

Mitzi, Beth's grandmother, who had been sitting at their big farm table, chopping nuts for her famous cinnamon rolls, which she planned to make for breakfast before the wedding the next day, looked up and raised an eyebrow.

Around her, the windows of the kitchen were all decorated with beautiful swags of juniper and pine—the same beautiful Victorian touch her mother always decorated the house with, but done up this year, Beth could tell, with a special flair. The tree in their living room, though, Beth had been glad to see, was just as it had always been: full of the delicate glass ornaments that her mother had collected year after year, everywhere they went, and that her father had added to by giving her mother a new ornament every year. Their tree was always a glistening, perfect gem, and she knew that, whatever else Gloria might take issue with in this wedding, even Gloria wouldn't be able to look down her nose at her mother's tree.

"Nadine," Gloria said, stepping forward to air kiss her on either side of Beth's mother's face. When they had first met, Nadine had tried to return the kisses, as a good Midwesterner, but by now she'd learned simply to hold still and let Gloria perform her ritual.

Beth glanced at the little Louis Vuitton satchel Ken had been carrying for Gloria as he set it gently down on the large black and white kitchen tiles. Her mother was exactly right. It was far tinier than anything anyone would expect Gloria Allerton to travel with, especially to her son's wedding. And that was because there was a huge pile of luggage waiting behind them in the front foyer.

Because Nadine couldn't seem to stop staring at it, Gloria deigned to give it a glance herself.

"Oh, that," she said. "It's just my dress. For the ceremony."

"Oh!" Beth's mother said, delighted to have a point of connection with Gloria. That didn't happen all that often in conversations between Nadine, who had spent her life as a farmer's wife in rural Michigan, and Gloria, who was one of the doyennes of the New York society scene. But both of them had children getting married tomorrow. And both of them had been on a hunt to find a suitable dress. "What did you wind up getting?"

"Oh, it's nothing special," Gloria said. "I mean, we are out here in the country. With all this snow," she said, looking out at the drifts beyond the windows as if the local servants couldn't really be trusted to clean things up the way the ones in the city did. "It's just something simple I picked up in Nice. Dove-gray French silk. Not too fancy, because I'm only going to cover it up with one of my mother's stoles. The fox is my favorite, but mother always said it was bad luck to wear fur with a face to a wedding. So I just brought her old ermine."

"Oh," Nadine said. Beth knew that her mother had been thrilled to find her own dress, an emerald chiffon that picked up her mother's green eyes, on a huge end-of-summer discount sale at the local mall—which was almost an hour away from town. But instead of saying anything about it, Nadine just clasped her hands together.

"When I got married . . ." Mitzi announced loudly, as Beth's heart sank. This had been her grandmother's favorite refrain, ever since Jen had started to bring in the preparations for the wedding in earnest in the last few weeks. And somehow, the comparisons she made were never to the advantage of Beth's own wedding.

But now both Gloria and Ken were looking at Mitzi with interest, which Mitzi observed with satisfaction. "I got married at noon, and we had cookies and lemonade in the church basement, and had to be out by two so they could start cooking their spaghetti supper," Mitzi declaimed. "And we were married sixty-three years."

Usually, this last announcement, of the extreme length of Mitzi's union with Jack, Beth's grandfather, resulted in oohs and aahs from whoever was listening, but Gloria and Ken both just looked slightly uneasy.

That didn't stop Mitzi. "You remember," she insisted to Gloria. "Weddings used to be simpler, didn't they?"

Gloria shrugged. "That's what I wanted," she said. "But then the count insisted that we use his summer palace. And he was such good friends with Daddy that Daddy said we couldn't really say no. I just wanted something simple, at home. Maybe just go down to Saint Patrick's, and then have dinner at the Plaza."

Beth watched her mother's eyes widen as Gloria spoke, name-checking two of the most famous landmarks anywhere in New York City, but Mitzi remained cucumber cool.

"All this hoopla," she said, waving her hand around in a fashion that could indicate the contents of the kitchen, or encompass the entire town. She shook her head wearily. "It won't help you if you've got the right person—or if you don't," she said, with another raise of an eyebrow. "I never saw any reason to turn the whole town upside down just because two kids are getting married. As if that never happened once before in the course of history."

Beth could see Ken trying to suppress a smile. But her grandmother's words still stung. Maybe it was the stress of the wedding. Maybe it was that she hadn't gotten a full night's sleep in days. But before she knew it, hot words had come to her lips. "You know, Grandma," she said, "it wasn't my idea to have this wedding here and upend everything. When we first got engaged, I thought we'd get married in New York City."

As soon as she said it, her mother's face dropped—and so did Beth's heart. It had been her mother's idea to have the wedding at home in Michigan. The ostensible reason was Mitzi—that it might be hard for her to travel to the big city, although Beth privately feared a lot more for anyone in the city who looked at Mitzi the wrong way than she feared for Mitzi.

But the real reason was that her mother hated having the wedding without Beth's father there. It had been almost three years now, but the idea of doing the wedding without him, in a strange place, where there were no reminders of their life together, was just too much for Nadine. It made the wedding more complicated in every way—although it wasn't as expensive, which meant that Nadine could keep a bit of her pride by contributing to the cost, which would have been impossible with a New York setting, at least of the kind that the Allertons would expect.

Still, in all their planning, Beth had never come right out and said what she'd just said, aloud. And when she saw the look on her mother's face, she knew why. Her mother looked hurt and lost. Even Mitzi, who didn't have much patience with people's little problems, looked at Nadine with sympathy, because she could see the look on her face came from genuine pain.

Quickly, Beth crossed the kitchen to give her mom a hug. "I mean," she said as her mother's arms wrapped around her, "but then I thought about it. And it only made sense to do it here."

Her mother gave her a squeeze to let her know that everything was forgiven.

"I can't believe I haven't offered you anything to drink!" her mother said to cover over the uncomfortable moment. She looked at the Allertons. "Can I get you anything? Water? Hot chocolate? Are you hungry? Would you like something to eat?"

Beth suppressed her reaction, knowing that what Ken Allerton probably wanted most right now was a good stiff drink, and that Gloria, to preserve her rail-thin figure, rarely ate anything at all.

Gloria offered some kind of simulation of a smile. "Oh, don't worry about me," she said. Then she looked around. "But where is Tom?"

"Over at the men's club," Mitzi said. This was what she had started calling Jen's house next door, which was where the groomsmen were staying before the wedding, to make sure there was no bad luck in terms of the bride and groom crossing paths the next morning before the appointed hour.

A hopeful expression crossed Gloria's face, probably at the possibility that there might actually be a men's club in this godforsaken backwater. But it was quickly followed by confusion, at the fact that there couldn't possibly be one that was up to her standards, this far from the city.

"He's staying next door," Nadine explained. "At the Fitzgeralds'."

"Oh," Gloria said. "The one who's planning the wedding."

"She's an old friend of mine," Beth said.

"He wants some hot chocolate," Mitzi said, pointing at Ken. "Don't you?"

"You know what?" Ken said. "I think I will."

Gloria shook her head wearily, as if this was just the most recent in an endless series of inexplicable decisions on her husband's part.

"Dear," she said to Beth, as Nadine turned to warm a pot of milk, "could you just show me to our room?"

"Of course!" Beth said. "It's this way."

As she headed out the kitchen door, she hesitated, looking into the entryway piled with luggage.

"Would you like me to bring . . . ?" she began, but Gloria waved the suggestion away.

"No, no," she said. "They'll bring it up later."

Beth didn't argue, but as they ascended the stairs, she wondered exactly who Gloria thought the mysterious "they" was who would be dragging her bags up the stairs later: Beth's mother? Mitzi? She'd have to do it herself once she got Gloria safely in her room, and just make sure Gloria didn't see her.

The room they'd selected for Gloria and Tom was their guest room, which doubled as Nadine's quilting nook. Beth's mother had bought new curtains for the occasion, and washed the antique quilt that covered the queen-sized bed, but Gloria dropped her bag on it with hardly a second glance.

"Dear," she said, pulling the scarf from her ash-blond hair and shaking it out. "I have something I want to give to you."

Beth could feel her heart thrum. Surprises, where Gloria was concerned, weren't always good ones. But probably, she told herself, this shouldn't have come as a surprise. The Allerton family was dripping with heirlooms. Of course Gloria would want to pass one on to her, if only to make it clear how many she had to spare.

Beth just hoped that it wouldn't be so flashy she couldn't wear it without distracting from the dress and jewelry she'd already chosen for her wedding day—or so expensive or historical that she couldn't wear it without being in a state of constant fear.

"Oh," Beth said. "Thank you."

"Don't thank me yet," Gloria said, turning around to dig through her bag.

But when she turned back, to Beth's surprise, she was holding a sheaf of paper.

"What's this?" Beth asked, confused.

"It's a prenuptial agreement," Gloria said.

"Tom and I aren't signing one of those," Beth said.

"That's what Tom said," said Gloria. "But I'm sure you have more sense than him. After all, you're the one who really understands the value of money."

"Because I don't have as much as Tom?" Beth said, trying to keep her voice steady.

"It's hard to know how much a thing is worth when you've never had to worry about it," Gloria said. "Which is why I'm worrying about this for him. I want you think about it this way, my dear. What could be more romantic than signing this? That way, you'll never have to worry whether he's staying with you for love, or because he's afraid of what he might lose if he left. You'll always know he's there for you and you only—for as long as he stays."

The way she said it made it sound as if she wasn't at all sure how long that would be.

Beth gazed at Gloria in shock.

"And he'll know the same thing about you," Gloria added. She folded the papers back to reveal a signature page, and held them out.

Beth could feel hot blood rise in her face, but at the same time she felt frozen in place.

"I'm not signing that," she said.

Gloria just smiled. "We'll talk more at the rehearsal dinner," she said as Beth backed out the door and fled down the hall.

Five

"YOU WOULD NOT BELIEVE the traffic here," Winston grumbled, his deep voice indistinct over the connection with Jen's cell phone. It sounded as if the signal was getting lost in the light snow that had started to fall since Jen had succeeded in convincing him to take the giant van he normally used for his tree-trimming business on an emergency run to collect the New Yorkers from the airport.

It was an old military troop transport truck that he'd picked up at some kind of sale that only people like Winston ever seemed to hear about. And although it was especially fragrant with the fresh smell of pine, because it had been very recently used to haul around the branches and trunks of actual pine trees, it had seating around the sides for almost twenty, with plenty of room still left for their luggage, which Winston insisted on referring to as "gear."

Jen had talked him into making the run through a combination of quavery-voiced pleas and references to a number of favors she'd done him during the years since they'd become best buds in high school while both playing trombone in the school band. Most of those involved bringing him by an extra pie or casserole when she'd made something for the family, since he lived at the next farm down the road from hers, and had been all alone there since his dad died, a few years after they graduated from high school. The two of them had been alone out there together since his mama died when Winston was a boy, and as a result, the whole town kind of took him under their wing, with all kinds of people stopping by from time to time, to bring him all kinds of things. By now, he probably knew how to cook for himself, but nobody in the town had really gotten that through their heads yet.

But the real clincher had been when Jen began to hint at the most profound favor she'd ever done for him: going on a double date with him and his first-ever Internet date. Winston had been all slicked up and wearing his best shirt, but the girl had turned out to be so high-maintenance she looked like she was born with a manicure. She was insulted from the moment that she walked in the door that he hadn't "dressed" for their date, and things went downhill from there. By the time the four of them had parted ways, Winston had promised again and again that he owed her and Ed—and owed them big.

In the year since, Jen had never referred to it once. But when she'd started to turn the conversation in that direction, Winston had folded immediately. "Don't say it," he'd told her. "I'm getting my keys."

But now, though, the slick roads of southeastern Michigan seemed to have chilled his gratitude somewhat.

"This is why I never go to the city," he groused.

"Winston," Jen said reasonably. "You are not in the city. The Detroit airport is half an hour outside the city limits."

"Not far enough," Winston said darkly. "Now, which terminal did you tell me?"

"McNamara," Jen said quickly. "They're all coming into the big, new one."

"Got it," Winston said.

"Call me when you've got everyone?" Jen asked.

"If I make it that far," Winston said, and hung up.

Jen slid her phone back into her back pocket, looked around, and sighed.

The rehearsal dinner was over at the Deans' farm. They'd given up an active farming operation when Mr. Dean passed away, so another neighboring farmer was tilling the land, but the Dean barn wasn't in use anymore. It was smaller than the Fitzgeralds'—not big enough for a wedding party their size. But it was beautiful, with a large, wide hayloft that was still sturdy enough to host the two long tables Jen was having set up there for the catering staff who were serving the rehearsal dinner that night. And holding the dinner there was another way to help Beth feel like she was really having her wedding celebration at home, since she'd come back all this way just to do that.

"Where am I?" a gruff voice asked behind her.

Jen turned around with a smile to see her father, wearing just a black-and-red buffalo check shirt and a down vest despite the cold, his white hair even whiter at the tips because of the snow that had settled in it on the short walk over.

"I thought I was coming over to find my daughter at the Dean barn. But it looks like I stumbled into the Taj Majal."

"What do you think, Daddy?" Jen asked.

She already knew what her dad thought about the whole idea of getting married in a barn, especially in the middle of winter: People were crazy! They were willing to pay tens of thousands of dollars for the privilege of inviting all their friends to spend an afternoon in what Jen's father wouldn't stop pointing out was basically a horse house.

From the start, he had been skeptical that people who could be convinced to pay the rates Jen claimed she could get with a wedding business would have enough common sense not to accidentally knock the place over, or burn it down. If they were willing to pay thousands of dollars to spend the night in a barn, who knew what else they might be capable of?

Furthermore, he pointed out in case Jen hadn't noticed, he was still a working farmer. What did Jen propose to do with his livestock while she was hosting weddings in his barn? Put them up at the local Sheraton? Had the world turned completely upside down?

But Jen was barn proud. Not one of the barns she'd seen in any of the big, glossy magazines, and not one of the several barns she'd actually been forced to enter in a formal dress on the occasion of her own friends' weddings, held a candle to her family's barn, in her humble opinion. To Jen, that sounded like an opportunity.

And in Beth, she had the perfect first customer. The two of them had dreamed about getting married in the barn since they were both little girls. And Beth had been trying to deal with the crazy expectations of her rich in-laws-to-be ever since she'd started dating Tom—and with disappointing them.

"Nothing I ever do is going to be fancy enough for Gloria Allerton," Beth had told Jen in their planning conversations. "So all I can do is be myself. I don't want to get married in one of these giant old palaces for the rich and famous in New York. I want to get married at home." Since her father had died just a few years ago, she didn't want her mother to feel out of place and alone in some fancy cathedral or hotel ballroom. And even if she felt like putting her mother through it, her grandmother Mitzi was getting too fragile to travel—although she was so spunky she would never have admitted that herself.

Plus, having the wedding at home meant it was something that the Deans could afford to pay for themselves, which to Beth, and to her mother, meant a lot. "Gloria's always thought I was after Tom's money," Beth had told Jen. "When actually, some- times I think I'd like him better if he just had a regular job like everyone else." To Beth, having her family pay for the wedding, as tradition usually dictated, was an important way to keep the Dean family's dignity as they merged their lives with the seemingly much more powerful Allertons.

At first, the Allertons had been on board with the idea of a destination wedding, even at Christmas. The family had never had much of a home Christmas tradition themselves, with the holidays celebrated by trips all over the world, from Shanghai to Ibiza. So Gloria had thought at first that if what Beth wanted was a destination wedding, it ought to be a simple thing to talk Beth into a much more interesting destination than rural Michigan.

She'd started, according to Beth's reports to Jen, by trying to tempt Beth with other locations: historic churches in Italy or Greece, or lush garden spots so exclusive no one who hadn't been to them had ever heard of them. When she'd realized Beth wasn't budging, she'd started in on the whole idea of getting married in a barn "in the dead of winter," as she liked to refer to it: how cold it was going to be, how inconvenient without suitable seating, how distant from any kind of food that any civilized person might actually want to eat.

Both Beth and Jen knew all of these concerns were groundless. Both of their fathers had been good farmers, which meant that the barns on their properties, even though they still had the old lines of the original wood, had long ago been buttoned up tight with modern caulking and insulation against the cold, with electricity installed so they could have light to work by night and run heat when the temperatures dropped too low. And in both barns, they'd also long ago poured sturdy cement floors, suitable for being cleaned within an inch of their life for guests, and smooth enough to serve as either banquet hall or dance floor.

"What's funny," Beth had told Jen, "is that she hasn't ever

thought to complain about the fact that actual animals still live there. I don't think that possibility's even crossed her mind."

And as Jen listened to her, she was always reminded of how much Gloria Allerton's arguments against a barn wedding sounded like her own father's.

Patiently, Jen had pointed out to her father that since Mr. Dean, on the next farm down, had passed away a few years ago, Mrs. Dean had her hands full just wrangling Mitzi, her mother-in-law, whose feistiness hadn't been dampened even a whit by her eighty-plus years. They'd given up most of their livestock, and Mrs. Dean had said she'd be grateful for the income whenever Jen wanted to board any of their own stock there—which would literally just mean walking them less than an acre from one barn to the next.

But it wasn't really the affordability, or the ease, or even the hominess, that had made both Beth and then Jen fall in love with the idea of a barn wedding—yes, even in the dead of winter. It was the sheer magic of it. No church, no matter how beautiful, would ever have the charm of the rough-hewn wood beams of a well-loved barn, especially one whose roof you'd grown up under. No red carpet into a fancy hotel would ever match the grandeur of the carpet of white that God threw over the world for free in Michigan every winter. And no homecoming or gathering of friends was ever as sweet as one that came at Christmas.

But despite the magic, and the undeniable sense of the plans Jen kept pestering her family with, her dream business might never have gotten off the ground if it weren't for Beth. Jen's father could say no to Jen all day long. He'd gotten lots of practice with that during her growing-up years, when she'd wanted to try everything in the world, from roller-skating down their usually deserted country road, to trying on Mitzi's lipstick, which came in many shades of *far too bright*.

But he'd always had a soft spot in his heart for Beth, ever since she and Jen had grown up together—born the same year, and in the same grade at school. In fact, Jen's mother whispered to her, the way he always seemed to spoil Beth was the way he would have spoiled Jen, if Jen's mom hadn't given him more than one good talking-to.

And when Beth had fallen in love with the idea of the Christmas barn wedding, and gone to Jen's father to beg his permission, he hadn't been able to resist.

But was he regretting that now? Jen wondered. Or—she barely dared to let even a corner of her heart have the slightest hope—was there some chance that what she had pulled off in the barn today had changed his mind about the whole idea, even just a little?

"I think it's amazing what people will pay good money for," her father said. "For example, there's a boy down there in my front yard with a whole truckload of champagne. Wants to know where to put it. I assume you don't want it in the barn overnight, unless you're planning on serving it as shaved ice."

"Oh," Jen said, heading for the stairs that led down from the loft. "I'll come right over."

Her phone rang for the second time just as the kid with the champagne finished loading the last case into her parents' hurricane basement, which was warm enough to keep the champagne chilled but unfrozen, and provided a very handy entrance and exit for loading and unloading.

"I've got them all," Winston said over the line. "We're heading home."

"Winston," Jen said. "How are they doing?"

"Well," Winston said. "You know. I had one gentleman who was very insistent he get some whiskey. Seemed to think my truck was a low-flying private jet."

"Just tell him we've got top-shelf here," Jen said. "As soon as he—"

"I gave him some," Winston said.

"You had whiskey in your truck?" Jen yelped, incredulous.

"This is a full-service tree service, ma'am," Winston said.

"I don't want to know where you keep it, do I?" Jen asked.

"Probably not," Winston said.

In the background, Jen could hear a woman talking.

"Who's that?" Jen asked. "What's she saying?"

"That," Winston said, "is Sylvia."

From his tone, Jen could tell that Sylvia, who she knew was a member of the bridal party, was already on his last nerve.

"By the time Sylvia found the truck," Winston went on, "all the jump seats in the back were taken. So she is riding up front with me."

"Best seat in the house!" Jen could hear Sylvia crow over the line, her voice tinny with the distance from the phone.

"Winston," Jen said. "You realize it's not just your job to bring them back. You also have to bring them back unharmed."

Winston chuffed indignantly on the other end of the phone. "You've got it all backwards," he said. "It's *my* health you should be worrying about."

"I think he'd prefer a truckload of trees," Sylvia called from the next seat, her voice raised for Jen's benefit.

"Trees don't talk so much," Winston shot back.

Because neither of them could see her, Jen allowed herself the luxury of a grin.

"Okay," she said. "I'm going to let you go so you can concentrate on your driving. And," she added, just to tweak Winston a bit, "your conversation."

"We're not just even after this," Winston warned. "You're going to owe me."

"We'll negotiate," Jen told him, and clicked off the line.

By the time she did, she had to brush snow off her phone. When she'd checked the weather report that morning, a substantial snow had been predicted for later in the day—but not until after night fell. She'd told herself that would be fine—the guests would all be snug in their various accommodations by then, and when they woke, there'd be a fresh blanket of white over everything—almost as if Jen had ordered it up for the wedding.

But this was a good six hours before she expected to see her first flake. And this was hardly a light flurry. The world around her looked more like a snow globe than a postcard, the air full of thick flakes, which were sticking instead of melting away, because there was already snow on the ground.

She opened the weather app on her phone and checked the map. The small squall that had been lurking over Chicago earlier that morning had now grown to a full-fledged storm, and the leading edge of it had already crossed over into Michigan.

Quickly, Jen checked the projected accumulation. It was about twice as much as they'd reported before as well: almost ten inches, in addition to what was already on the ground. But when she scrolled to the bottom of the page to check the hourly weather until the next morning, she breathed a sigh of relief. The skies should be clear in time for the wedding.

That was if, she suddenly realized, this report was accurate. Which the one she had read six hours ago apparently hadn't been.

As she started to slip the phone in her back pocket again, it began to vibrate and ping.

When she raised it to her ear, she caught sight of an out-of-town number, and one she didn't recognize. Was one of the guests from Winston's van already so outraged by the accommodations that they were calling to complain?

She took a deep breath and answered.

"Hey," the man's voice on the other end of the line said.

It only took that word for her to recognize the voice: Jared. And it only took a moment more for a feeling of warmth and familiarity to wash over her—almost as if she had just walked in the door of her own parents' house.

Jen bit her lip.

"Is this the line for the Fitzgerald wedding?" Jared asked.

"Yes," Jen said. Would he recognize her voice?

Apparently not by a single word. "Okay, great," Jared said. "Listen, I'm really sorry to bug you, but my mom and my sister and everyone are up to their ears with this wedding. And I think I just missed my ride from the airport. There was supposed to be some kind of bus, but my plane just landed. I ran all the way out to the meeting place, but there's no one else from the wedding there. And the invitation said I should call this number."

Over the past few years, Jen had imagined a thousand ways that their next conversation might go. She'd always known they'd have another one. It was impossible they wouldn't cross paths again, living next door, with her so close to his sister. But of all the options she had dreamed up, she had never thought it would go like this.

He still didn't have any idea he was even talking with her.

And for the moment, she suddenly decided, she was just going to keep it that way.

"All right," she said, doing her best to make her voice sound like some professional on a customer service line. "I'll see what I can do."

Six

BETH HADN'T EVEN THOUGHT to take a coat with her when she slipped out of her mother's house, by the front door instead of the back one that opened off the kitchen, so that she wouldn't have any chance of running into her mother, or Mitzi, or Ken Allerton.

When she got outside, she was surprised by how much snow had already begun to fall, but by that point, nothing could have induced her to go back into that house and run the risk of having to confront Gloria again, too.

And the mild sting of snow on her face felt good. It gave her something to feel besides the ache and dread that had begun in her heart as soon as she realized what was on the document that Gloria had been waving in her face. And as each flake melted on her cheeks and forehead, it gave her a sense that she still had some kind of power—power enough at least to melt snow down to dew with her own heat and to survive the chill, even without a jacket.

Besides, the walk was short, less than a hundred steps between the two houses, through the ragged lilac hedge, on a path that had already been trampled into the original snow, before this new batch began to fall. And it was so familiar that she could have done it in her sleep. She practically had in her younger days, when she and Jen had swapped sleepover nights as girls or tiptoed through the country darkness as teenagers to swap secrets.

But by the time she came up the back steps to the Fitzgeralds' kitchen, she was shivering.

And when she stepped inside, Tom, who had been leaning against a counter, nursing a cup of coffee, looked up at her in shock. Beside him, the giant green felt Christmas elf that was presiding over Mrs. Fitzgerald's counter for the season echoed his surprise.

"Hey, sweetheart," he said, laying the coffee cup aside and coming over to wrap her in a hug. "Haven't you ever heard of a coat?" he asked, burying his face in her hair.

For a long moment, Beth just let herself sway against him. From the first time he'd put his arms around her, he'd seemed to have some magic power to block out the rest of the world and make her feel safe and protected, as if there were nobody else in it but them.

But now, after the brief respite of his embrace, the rest of the world began to rush in again: not just all the details of the wedding, but the throbbing hurt of the papers his mother had just been pushing her to sign.

Beth gave him a tight squeeze but then began to squirm out of his arms.

As she did, he grinned, then began to bat at her hair and shoulders, brushing snow away in flurries that settled into glistening piles on the scuffed tile, then quickly melted in the warmth of the kitchen.

"This is some kind of Midwestern beauty ritual, right?" he said with a grin. "The prewedding snow-pack facial?"

Tom looked at her so innocently, and with such joy and goodwill, that Beth felt another twist in her gut: both of anger at Gloria, for intruding with her crazy ideas on what was supposed to be Beth and Tom's beautiful day, but also of dread, that she was going to have to spoil Tom's happy mood—and once she did, she didn't know when either of them would feel so carefree and hopeful again.

But in the meantime, she tried to joke along. "We're not the gullible ones smearing old charcoal on our faces, out in the country," she said. "That's the city folk. But I should let Jen know about a snow facial. Maybe she can sell it to some of our New York friends for two hundred bucks a pop."

"A hundred bucks if she brings a bucket of fresh snow to their room," Tom said. "Two hundred bucks for the privilege of going out and planting their own face in the snow themselves."

"They do like it when they have to do things for themselves," Jen agreed.

"That's because it's such a novelty for them," Tom said. Then he raised his hand, to indicate he wasn't done declaiming. "As long as it doesn't involve any actual work. They'll pay you a hundred bucks to do a workout with bricks for hand weights. But if they want actual bricks laid, someone else is gonna have to do that. For a lot less than a hundred bucks an hour."

Beth tried to smile, but without much success, her eyes sliding away from his and focusing on the string of colored lights hung from the curtain rod over the Fitzgeralds' kitchen sink. For some reason they were in the shape of icicles and also blinked in time with the tinny Christmas carols leaking faintly from the kitchen radio.

But Tom, who often caught expressions that she wasn't even aware she'd made, caught this one.

"Hey, babe," he said, trying to pull her close again. "What's wrong?"

Beth knew that she couldn't have the conversation she needed to have if she was wrapped up with him. She needed to see his face so that she could gauge his reaction to what she was about to say: Did some part of him secretly agree with his mother? Or not so secretly? So she pulled away as he reached for her.

And then the look on his face made her heart do another sick backflip.

She reached for his hand and held it in both of her own.

"So cold," Tom said.

"I'm sorry," she said. "It's just . . ."

To her chagrin, tears began to roll down her cheeks. She hadn't wanted to cry, she thought angrily. She had wanted to discuss this calmly, in a grown-up fashion, the way they'd agreed they'd try to handle conflicts in their marriage.

She squeezed her eyes shut in frustration. Their marriage hadn't even started yet, and here she was, already dissolving at the first sign of trouble.

Then she felt a gentle touch on her cheek. It was Tom, actually wiping away the tears from the corners of her eyes, erasing their tracks down her face.

"Babe," he said with a smile. "You've got to tell me. Did something go wrong with the plans? We don't have the right kind of snapdragons? You know none of that matters to me, as long as I wind up with you at the end of—"

"It's your mother," Beth blurted.

"Mom?" Tom repeated.

For a moment, confusion covered his face. But then she could see a dawning realization that let her know he already had some growing inkling of what she was about to say.

Still, it was hard for her to say it out loud. When she'd spoken with Gloria, she'd refused to have anything to do with the papers. It was almost as if she thought that if she ignored them, she could erase them. But talking about it with Tom, saying the words out loud—somehow that felt like it was making everything too real. The words to Tom were the ones she could never take back, the ones they'd have to live with all their lives.

She bowed her head under the weight of it.

"She didn't," Tom said, his voice suddenly full of fury.

Beth looked up. She saw nothing but righteous indignation in his face—no trace of hesitation or doubt. When he reached for her this time, she allowed him to gather her up in his arms.

"I told her not to say a word about that to you," Tom said. "I told her to tear them up."

"Well, she didn't," Beth said.

"Honey," Tom said, kissing her cheek. "Sweetheart. I'm so sorry. She had no right."

Then his hands, which had been gently stroking her back, suddenly froze, as if arrested by a thought.

"What did you tell her?" he asked.

Beth took a deep breath and pulled away again, so they could see each other. "I told her no," she said.

Tom nodded firmly. "That's right," he said. "I wouldn't expect anything less."

"She said she'd talk with me about it later," Beth said, trying to control the quaver that came to her voice as she did. Why did dealing with Gloria make her feel like such a little kid? And not in the good way—protected and hopeful. But like a kid who nobody wanted around, and who could never figure out what the right thing to do or say was.

"I'll talk to her," Tom said, setting his jaw.

Beth felt a wave of gratitude, but also a pang. He looked like he was readying himself for battle, but it was the night before their wedding. She didn't want the two of them starting their life together with a huge fight between Tom and his mom—especially not one over her.

"If you really want me to," Beth said softly, "I would sign it."

As she said this, her eyes filled with tears, blurring the image of the giant lit tree outside the window into a thick white triangle of light.

"Absolutely not," Tom said instantly, as if he was dismissing an insulting offer out of hand from one of the dozens of businesses that he and his father bought and sold and sometimes managed. "She should never have even asked you the question. We shouldn't even be talking about it right now. We should be doing something else, like . . ."

For a moment, his expression softened, and he drew Beth in for a kiss.

But even before their lips parted, they both knew they weren't through with the conversation.

"But we are talking about it," Beth pointed out. "And I don't want to see you have some big blowout with your mother the night before our wedding. Who knows how long it will take for her to cool down? It could be years."

"She should have thought of that," Tom said, "before she tried to make you sign a prenup. After I expressly asked her not to."

"I know," Beth said. "But she did. So maybe . . ." she said, surprised at where her own thoughts were taking her. "Maybe it doesn't matter that much if I sign it," she said. "We're going to be married forever. Or at least till death do us part."

Tom looked at her, bemused. "You're going to trade me in for a better model when we get to heaven?" he asked.

"I might just take a look at what's available," Beth said, with a wink. "But in that case, who cares whether we have a prenup or not? If we never break up, it won't ever matter."

"We're never breaking up," Tom said.

"And I don't want to start out this marriage with your mother furious at me," Beth added.

Tom watched her for a long minute. He took a deep breath. "You'd really do that?" he asked.

Beth nodded.

Tom shrugged. "If you really want to, I won't stop you," he said.

But at these words, all the disbelief and anger Beth had felt when she first realized what Gloria was asking her to do rose up in her again.

She hadn't thought she was testing Tom. But until his steady resolve not to have anything to do with the prenup crumbled, she hadn't realized how much she needed it from him.

"Really?" she asked. "Would that really be all right with you?"

Tom's eyes widened at the change in her. "Honey," he said. "I didn't say it would be all right. I said if you *wanted*—"

But Beth held her hand up, cutting him off. "You know what?" she said. "I think it's better if we don't talk about this right now."

Tom tried to reach for her hand. "But then when are we going to talk about it?" he asked.

Beth slipped away from him, heading for the door.

"You're not going to go out again without a coat," Tom said. "The snow's so thick you can barely even see Jen's house."

Beth looked out into the white flakes beyond the windows, which were coming so fast now she couldn't even see the lilac hedge just a few steps beyond the kitchen. Somehow the roiling weather seemed like a mirror of her own heart.

"I've got stuff I need to do for Jen," she said. "I don't have time to deal with this right now."

As she reached for the door, she realized the irony: she was telling her groom that she didn't have time to talk about their marriage, because she was too busy with their wedding.

But that didn't stop her from walking out.

Seven

JEN PULLED INTO THE crawling line of airport traffic and tried unsuccessfully to take a deep breath.

If she'd been able to think of any other way to get Jared back from the airport than picking him up herself, she would have done it. But she was afraid she was going to have to trade away her hypothetical firstborn child to Winston in order to get him to make a return trip. Even if he did, they were so close to the actual rehearsal that if Winston took the time to drop off everyone else and then come back, Jared wouldn't make it back to join the wedding party in time. And she didn't want to have Winston try to turn the van around and return to the airport with all the other guests still with him. The less time Beth's New Yorkers had to spend amidst the tree-trimming equipment, the better.

Jen's mom was still at work, and her dad was busy taking care of the horses, who were still going to stable overnight in their barn, so the Deans' loft would be creature-free for the rehearsal dinner. Then he'd walk them over to the Deans' early tomorrow morning so the Fitzgerald barn would be free of livestock for the wedding itself. She thought about sending Mackenzie Becket, a local high school student who was going to be helping her with the details at the rehearsal and the wedding. But she didn't want to be responsible for sending a brand-new driver out into the midst of what was quickly becoming a minor blizzard. And Mackenzie wasn't due to show up for duty for another few hours.

So when Jen got off the phone with Jared, she'd run a quick calculation on how fast she could get to the airport and back. If she left now, she realized, she could be back within an hour of the time the other guests arrived—and still with a reasonably healthy margin before the rehearsal began.

But now, in the moments before she was going to have to see Jared, she couldn't help second-guessing the decision. She'd steeled herself for the pang of sorrow or even anger, both of which she'd felt a lot of since the last time she saw him, when he went off to take his big new energy industry job down in Texas.

What she hadn't been prepared for was what she was feeling now: anticipation. To her surprise and chagrin, she felt just like she always had when she was going to pick him up from the airport—all those years when he'd been coming home from school, or some trip, and she'd gone to get him—and all those years when he'd dropped her off or picked her up under the same old airport overhang.

Annoyed, she tried to push the feeling away, scanning the crowd for Jared's familiar figure.

She'd gotten a new number to keep her business calls separate from her personal, and since he'd first called in, she'd simply been texting him, not ready yet to deal with whatever his reaction would be to seeing her again. So all he knew was that someone from the wedding was coming to pick him up in a red sedan. But she couldn't put off the moment of truth indefinitely.

The slow motion of the pickup line and the predictable curbside activity was almost hypnotic. Pull up a few feet. Watch another pair embrace: mom and daughter, granddad and grandson, happy couple. Pull up another few feet. It was a rhythm you couldn't hurry even if you wanted to, which made it feel like it could go on forever.

Then, suddenly, there he was. She wasn't sure if she picked him out of the crowd of hundreds by the unmistakable curls of his sandy brown hair, by his tall frame, or by the familiar way he stamped his feet and blew on his hands to ward away the cold.

But when she saw him, her heart gave a leap that was both familiar and strange: something it had done so many times before—but not in such a long time.

She took a deep breath, nosed the car up to the curb where he was standing, and popped the trunk. At the sight of her new red sedan, Jared gave a friendly nod and waved, but Jen could tell from his expression that he was blind to who was driving through the reflection of the windows. This was the face he showed to strangers, not the real smile that lit up his face at the sight of real family or friends.

"Okay," Jen muttered to herself, putting the car into park. "Let's do this."

She opened the door and stepped out of the car.

Jared, who had been whistling a few notes of what was immediately recognizable as "Deck the Halls" as he swung his bag into the trunk, broke off immediately.

Jen had imagined dozens of times what he would look like when they saw each other again, but none of them had ever been even remotely this satisfying. She'd imagined him looking sorry, or overjoyed, or ashamed of himself for being foolish enough to take off for Texas without her.

Instead, he looked as if he'd just been frozen to the ground by a powerful sorceress in some winter fairyland.

His bag dropped, forgotten, into her trunk. But his hand

didn't move to shut it. His mouth, which had dropped open, didn't close. And his eyes, which had gone wide, didn't blink.

Jen grinned.

"Surprise!" she said.

This seemed to be the magic word that broke the spell.

In answer to her grin, Jared's face broke out into one of the widest smiles she'd ever seen. Before she knew what was happening, he'd gathered her up in a bear hug that lifted her several feet off the ground before he did a half spin and deposited her again exactly where he had originally been standing.

"You stinker," Jared said, the elation in his voice belying his words. "You stinking stinker." Then realization dawned in his eyes. "Was that *you*?" he asked. "Who I talked to on the phone?"

Jen nodded.

Jared's grin only grew with delight over the fact he'd been duped. "Jen Fitzgerald," he said. "CIA operative."

Jen shook her head. "I'm a wedding planner," she said. "It's harder. And more dangerous."

Jared laughed. Then he cleared his throat, obviously trying to figure out where to start. "Wait, so what . . . ?" he began.

But Jen reached behind her and slammed the trunk shut.

"We can talk on the road," she said.

As she pulled back into the airport traffic, which picked up speed as they left the snarl of pickups behind them, a thousand thoughts spun through her mind about what to say next. Then a single thought stopped them all: she wasn't the only person in the car. And she wasn't the one who had broken up with Jared. Why shouldn't *he* be the one to figure out what to say next?

Almost as if he'd been listening in on her thoughts, Jared cleared his throat. "I hear you're planning this whole wedding," he said. "How's that going?"

It'd be a lot better if you hadn't missed the bus, Jen thought to herself. But there was no reason to start out with a snarky comment. So she just shrugged. "It's going okay," she said. "The hardest part has been trying to keep my mom's Christmas habit under control."

Jared laughed. Christmas decorations were a running joke, decades long, between people who knew the Dean and Fitzgerald families. Nadine Dean, everyone knew, had a prized collection of blown glass ornaments that might crack if anyone so much as looked at them, and only decorated her home with real, live swags of pine. But Mary, Jen's mother, had the Christmas sensibilities of a dime-store elf. From the day after Thanksgiving, their home exploded in Christmas lights, none of which matched and all of which seemed to blink, tchotchkes, the stranger the better, and what seemed to be an encyclopedic collection of every Christmas ornament ever made.

The only thing the two women agreed on taste-wise was their yearly codecoration of the giant pine between their two houses, which they always sent their husbands up on ladders with giant swags of white lights to decorate. And since Mr. Dean's passing, Winston had come over with his tree-trimming equipment to help Mr. Fitzgerald get the lights up, just like always.

Jen had tried to make some subtle suggestions to her mother about toning it down this year, since guests from the wedding would be staying with them who might not share the same enthusiasm for Christmas, since nobody but Mrs. Santa Claus herself could be expected to have that much Christmas enthusiasm.

But subtlety surrounding Christmas was not in her mother's vocabulary.

"Yeah?" Jared said. "How did that go?"

Jen shook her head. "I can't tell," she said. "Asking her to tone it down might have made it worse. But there was always so much Christmas junk in the house, it's kind of impossible to tell."

"Does she still have that velvet Santa?" Jared asked.

Jen smiled and nodded. When she was a girl, she'd fallen in love with a velvet Santa doll that, when she was six, was about the same height as her. She'd pounced on it at a garage sale and refused to leave without it. And since that level of decor fit right in with her mother's aesthetic, he'd been a central fixture of the Fitzgerald family Christmas ever since. "Yeah," she said. "I think the New Yorkers are gonna be really impressed by him."

After Jared's laugh at this, another awkward silence settled in between them, until Jared ventured, "So, what else have you been up to?"

"You mean, today?" Jen asked. "Or for the last three years?"

"Um," Jared said, shuffling in his seat. "Whatever."

At the discomfort she could hear in his voice, Jen relented. She gave him a quick rundown of what she'd been up to since he'd moved to Texas, making sure to highlight the parts that made it sound as if she was having an absolutely fabulous time without him: the fact that she was starting her own business, the trips she'd taken to California and London, the promotion she'd been given at her job at the hospital, where she'd started out in reception and was already office manager.

"Wow," Jared said. "That sounds more like ten years' worth of living than three."

"Are you saying I look old?" Jen said, glancing over to give him the stink eye.

"No," Jared said, his gaze taking in everything about her. "You look great, Jen."

She'd heard him give her enthusiastic comments before—

sometimes verbally, and sometimes with just a touch or a kiss. But this time, he sounded almost wistful.

Well, she thought to herself. *Whose fault is that?*

"What about you?" Jen asked. "What have you been up to?"

"Ah," Jared said. "I don't even know." But he immediately belied his statement with a detailed description of all his accomplishments, and his plots for the future: the way he'd worked his way up through three different positions in the company that had hired him, and just now been poached by another one, whose CEO had decided to hire him after Jared outnegotiated the company's representative in a deal Jared had been part of.

"You ever think about going to Texas?" Jared asked.

Jen almost laughed. She'd thought about it every day, for a long time. But he hadn't invited her. In fact, he'd made it quite clear he didn't want her slowing him down.

"How do you like it?" she asked, without answering his question.

"Well," Jared said. "It's beautiful. I mean, there's nothing like it. Even still today, there are times when I'm driving, especially in West Texas, when I think, *This can't be real. I must have driven onto a movie set while I wasn't looking.* The sky is so big. And the land is so wide."

"Sounds nice," Jen said in about the same tone of voice she would have if he were describing a new girlfriend to her.

Jared, catching something in her voice, looked over—and kept looking. "But I don't have much time to meet people," he said. "And the girls I do meet, well . . ."

Jen held on to the steering wheel as if she were suddenly driving through a much bigger storm than the light snowfall they were actually speeding through.

"Let's just say I'm not seeing anyone," Jared said.

What was the right answer to that? Jen wondered. Did he want her to feel sorry for him?

"So . . ." Jared said. "What about you?"

"What about me?" Jen repeated.

"I mean," Jared said, "have you been seeing anybody? I mean, I'm sure you must be seeing people. Unless all the guys in Blue Hill have gone blind. But . . . seeing anyone seriously?"

"I've been seeing someone for about a year," Jen said. "And it's going well. Very well," she added.

"Oh, wow!" Jared said, with what she immediately recognized as totally false enthusiasm. "That's great."

For a second the two of them sat in the most awkward silence they'd ever experienced together.

"Um," Jared said. "Do I know him?"

"It's Ed," she said.

"Ed?" Jared repeated.

"Ed Mason," Jen repeated, somewhat impatiently. There had only been one Ed in their graduating class. What other Ed could Jared think she was talking about?

Jared actually guffawed.

Jen looked at him, surprised.

Then Jared choked off his laughter, midguffaw.

"Wait," he said. "You're serious."

"Why wouldn't I be serious?" Jen asked. "Ed's a good guy. He's got a good job." *He wants to be with me*, she added in her head. *And furthermore, he doesn't live in Texas.*

"It's nothing," Jared said. "It's just that—"

"What?" Jen demanded.

"I don't know," Jared said. "I just remember that guy could never seem to make up his mind."

A wave of irritation rose up in Jen. That did actually drive her crazy about Ed. But what drove her even crazier was that Jared knew it.

"And doesn't he kind of hate to leave town?" Jared asked. "I remember we had tickets once to see the circus at the Cobo Hall and Mason was like, 'Everything I wanna see, I can see right here in Blue Hill.'"

By now, if Jen had been a cartoon character, smoke would have been leaking from her ears. Ed had said the same exact thing to her, approximately once a month, the entire time they'd been dating. But she agreed with him. She wanted to travel the world, but there was no place she'd rather live her real life than Blue Hill. Ed seemed reasonably interested when she told him about all the places she wanted to go. And besides, they weren't at a place yet where they needed to worry about traveling together. What right did Jared have to come swanning in here, criticizing her relationship, after he was the one who left her?

"I don't think it's really any of your business," Jen said, surprised by the curtness in her own voice.

"Okay, okay," Jared said, raising his hands in surrender. "I'm glad you two are happy."

We are? echoed in Jen's mind.

"There's a lot that's worth seeing in Blue Hill," she snapped.

Then the two of them sank into silence again.

And this time, it lasted for miles.

Eight

"SO, HOW DO YOU know Beth?" Sylvia tried, as another mile of snow-covered Michigan farmland slid by outside the sleet that ran sideways across her passenger-side window, blown by the force of motion of the truck, which had just turned off the freeway, at an exit that proclaimed *Blue Hill*.

Behind her, the other guests from New York, including a couple of her friends, chatted happily, but so far, all her attempts at starting a conversation with the grouchy lumberjack in the driver's seat had fallen flat.

"Almost there!" she'd chirped when they finally turned off the freeway after what seemed like an already interminable tour of billboards and flatland.

Instead of celebrating with her, the driver, who had at least let slip that his name was Winston, had only raised his eyebrows— not even at her, but at the snow falling outside the vehicle, as if it were some buddy of his at a bar who was sharing the moment with him of exactly how aggravating she was being.

"I guess that depends what you mean by 'almost,'" he'd said before sinking into the moody silences that had so far character-ized their whole drive together.

But this had only made Sylvia stubborn. It was a game of hers, even in the city, to win over the surliest and most stone-faced clerks she encountered, whether they were working a bodega or the cosmetics counter at Barneys—or the courts where she worked as a lawyer.

This guy was a real tough case, with a personality that was starting to seem more like the abominable snowman, rather than the gruff woodsman she'd figured him for when she'd first hopped in.

But she wasn't afraid of tough cases. And she didn't have anything better to do to pass the time.

From the look on his face now, though, she could tell that her question hadn't exactly been the magic conversational bullet she might have hoped for.

Winston's face wrinkled as if he'd just gotten a baby down for the night, settled into his favorite easy chair, and then heard the sound of a new wail from the darkened bedroom he'd just left behind.

"Um," he said, in a tone of voice obviously meant to let her know that only an absolute imbecile would have asked such a question.

But Sylvia was an expert at the use of silence in interrogation. He was waiting for her to retreat, to fill the empty conversational space for him. But she wasn't about to. And even a big bear like Winston couldn't bring himself to ignore her question completely—especially now that he'd already indicated, quite clearly, that he'd heard it.

"I don't know that I could tell you that," he said. "I've known Beth long as I can remember. Our mothers probably introduced us at some backyard barbecue back before either of us could even talk."

There was something sweet about the story, Sylvia thought, but nothing sweet about the way Winston told it. And as soon as he did, he sank back into an even moodier silence.

Most people loved to talk, Sylvia knew, so that was always her first line of attack. But it wasn't her only one. And if he didn't think he wanted to have a conversation, she was perfectly capable of producing one herself.

"I met her at a pro bono workshop," she said.

This caught Winston's attention. "Pro Bono?" he repeated. "You two big U2 fans?"

Sylvia didn't bother to correct his pronunciation. "It's a legal term. Free legal help, for people who can't afford it otherwise."

"Hm," Winston said, with slightly less rancor than he'd evidenced in the rest of the conversation.

"Beth was the lead on my first case with Legal Aid," Sylvia said. "But both of us were in over our heads. The big partners hardly do that kind of work anymore. A lot of it is kids just out of school, doing their best. On some of the hardest cases I've ever worked."

"What kind of case?" Winston asked.

It was the first question he'd asked her on the entire ride. And it was a far cry from *What kind of a moron are you?*, which was the question that had seemed to be on the tip of his tongue for most of that time.

"Lease case," Sylvia said. "Woman's husband had run out on her and her kid and left her with a lease she couldn't pay. She had a friend who she could move in with, but the landlord was trying to ruin her credit if she broke the lease. Even though it wasn't in her name."

"Did you get him?" Winston asked, with real curiosity now.

"Yep," Sylvia said, nodding with satisfaction at the memory. "But it took us two months. And you really get to know someone when you work with them that long."

"Beth and I had a pumpkin farm one fall," Winston said. "Her dad gave her an acre out behind the barn, and we planted it full of Halloween pumpkins. With a row of monsters in the back."

"Monsters?" Sylvia asked.

"The real big ones," Winston said, with an enthusiasm he hadn't shown so far, for anything. "Atlantic Giants. They get bigger than some of the kids we had coming out there to pick their pumpkins."

"You sell any of them?" Sylvia asked.

"Couple," Winston said. "The problem was, they got so big no one could lift them. By the end, we told people they could just have them if they could carry them out. But no one did."

He lapsed into silence again, but this time it didn't feel like an unfriendly one. And Sylvia wasn't about to let the opportunity slip away.

"You know," she said, "I introduced Beth and Tom."

"Eh?" Winston asked. But it wasn't a totally unfriendly sound.

Sylvia nodded. "Tom's one of my oldest friends," she said. "We didn't meet at a backyard barbecue, but it was kind of the same thing, for New York."

"Eh?" Winston repeated, which Sylvia decided to interpret as *Oh, what's that?*

"Apparently, I shared my raisins with him in line for our pre-school interview," Sylvia said.

"An interview?" Winston asked, his voice full of incredulity. "For preschool?"

This was obviously a path that was going to produce nothing but conflict, so Sylvia rattled on down the conversational track she had already started on. "It didn't even cross my mind to real-ize how perfect they'd be for each other, until Tom walked in the door at my Christmas party, and I thought, *I should make sure he gets a chance to talk with Beth.*"

"How come?" Winston asked. For the first time in the conversation, his voice wasn't unfriendly.

Encouraged, Sylvia took a deep breath. "You know how the rich can be . . . different from the rest of us."

Winston tilted his head, as if to indicate he was listening but not necessarily agreeing.

"Well," Sylvia said, "Tom's not. He can talk to anyone in the world. I've seen him have long conversations with cabdrivers, and executives, and old ladies in the park, and kids on the train. And Beth's the same way. A lot of times, you take a fancy lawyer into a pro bono case, and they don't have any idea how to really talk to the clients. Their lives are just so different. But Beth always just treated everybody as if they were exactly the same."

"That's because they are," Winston observed dryly.

Sylvia shrugged. "People always say that," she said. "But they don't act that way."

Winston tilted his own head to acknowledge the point.

"So it popped into my head to set them up," Sylvia went on. "But when Tom got to my party, he saw Beth before he even got his coat off. And when I got over to him, he was like, 'Who is that?' I was going to extract a promise to take me to drinks in exchange for an introduction, but before I could conclude the negotiation, Beth came up and asked when I was going to introduce her to my friend."

"Sounds like they made the introduction themselves," Winston said.

"That's what they think," Sylvia said. "But the fact of the matter is that they were too shy to ask for each other's numbers. So I had tickets early in the new year to go see *Amélie* on Broadway. I'd bought them six months out. But I told them both I couldn't go, and asked them both if they'd mind going with a friend of mine. So they both showed up at the theater that night, and— *Voilà!*"

Winston glanced over at her with something between wariness and respect.

Beyond the windows, the steady diet of snow-covered fields they'd been passing through had started to give way to more frequent barns, and now a handful of houses.

"Is this Blue Hill?" Sylvia asked.

Winston nodded.

"Great," Sylvia said, with feeling. "I can't wait to get a cup of coffee."

"You want to go to stop at the gas station?" Winston asked. "Or the bakery downtown?"

By now, his tone was almost solicitous, but Sylvia laughed. "That's cute," she said, waving her hand. "But I'm not going to mess with whatever the local definition of coffee is. You can just take me to Starbucks."

"We don't have a Starbucks," Winston said, the rancor in his voice now back in full effect.

Sylvia's mind began to race. Starbucks was a last-ditch option, something she'd already reckoned with and decided was worth the sacrifice, for the sake of celebrating her friends' wedding. But it hadn't even occurred to her that Blue Hill wouldn't even have a Starbucks as an option.

As she peered through the haze of snow, almost as if she expected a well-lit coffee shop full of well-sourced beans to emerge full blown on the side of the country road, the big yards of the houses they were passing turned into city lots. Suddenly they were in a neat downtown area, which she could see as soon as they entered was only a few blocks long, because the fields began again three blocks after the business district started.

In the first block, Winston pulled up outside a rambling Victorian mansion, clearly labeled *Blue Hill Inn*.

Without another word to Sylvia, he hopped out. A moment later, she heard the back of the truck open. Then guests began to stream up the steps of the inn, lugging their bags.

A moment later, Winston hopped back in the cab and heaved what was clearly a large sigh of relief.

Then he realized Sylvia was still there and started as if he'd just seen a ghost.

"This is the inn," he told her bluntly, which Sylvia interpreted as, *Why don't you get out of my truck, already?*

"I'm staying with Beth," Sylvia told him. "Out at the farm."

"Oh," Winston said. "That's on my way home."

Sylvia refrained from thanking him sarcastically for not making her walk the last however many miles alone in the snow, and they drove in absolute silence down the two remaining blocks of downtown, and out into the rolling fields.

After what seemed like a slice of eternity, they pulled into the drive of a big, beautiful red farmhouse, with a wide front porch.

"This is Beth's place?" Sylvia asked.

Winston's nod was so small it was almost imperceptible.

"It's so cute!" Sylvia exclaimed, but when the look on his face soured even further, she got the hint that he didn't think "cute" was an appropriate compliment for farmland.

As soon as the truck came to a stop, he bolted from the driver's seat and ran around the back to yank her luggage out, clearly less motivated by chivalry than by a passionate desire to have his truck all to himself again.

Sylvia figured out on her own how to get the unwieldy door handle to release, then slid down from the high seat, knocking her black pants and coat into the muddy, ice-caked side of the truck. When she righted herself, her Italian boots had disappeared in the snow, and her pants and jacket were both covered with mud.

For the first time since she'd met him, she thought she saw the hint of a smile on Winston's face.

"Don't worry," he said, handing her rollaway bag to her. "That'll come out clean with some water. You have water in New York, right?"

Nine

BETH TRAMPED THROUGH THE snow along the short path from Jen's place to hers, which was already getting packed down into a thick sheet of sleety slush by the foot traffic between the two houses in preparation for the dinner tonight and the wedding tomorrow.

The falling snow was so thick now that Beth couldn't see all the way down to the road, although the red of the barn where she'd be married the next day was still visible, screened with white. Just a few hours before, the barn had seemed like a treasure box to her, an enchanted place where only the best kind of magic could happen.

Now she just felt a sense of dread when she thought of it. What if this was never meant to be a magic weekend? What if something deeper than the magic and frippery of a wedding was being revealed to her, and just in time? Was she even meant to be married into a family that would treat her the way Tom's family was treating her? What if the whole point of all of this was to save her from making the biggest mistake of her life?

But even as she thought this, her heart twisted even more. She could stand the thought of not having the wedding, losing the deposits, even disappointing all the friends who had already traveled now to be with them. But she couldn't stand the thought of getting up tomorrow and not having Tom in her life.

On the other hand, some voice inside her whispered, was

Tom even who she thought he was? If he was willing to cave to his mother over something this important, would she be able to trust him to stand up to anyone, for anything, when she needed him? Would she feel this alone when she really needed him, for the rest of her life?

When she got to the short flight of steps that led up to the back porch, she hesitated. The last thing she wanted to do was face her mother, and Mitzi, and Ken, in the kitchen. But enough snow had fallen now that sneaking around to the front door would require a significant slog.

And, she suddenly realized, she was freezing now. Going inside might be the last thing her mind wanted to do, but the chill that had been creeping into her fingers and toes was now starting to clench around her whole body, and it turned out that her body had some opinions about that. In fact, her body was so unhappy about the cold that it didn't care what her mind thought about anything. It was going inside, no matter what anyone thought.

She tried to steel herself, as she went up the stairs, for whatever she found in the kitchen, working up fragments of stories about what she'd been doing over at Tom's, and why she was just fine now.

But when the door swung open, and she felt the welcome rush of warm air surround her, even hotter than it had felt before because of the freezing cold she'd just come out of, she was relieved to see that the only person left in the kitchen was her mom.

Almost immediately, though, Beth realized this might be even harder to deal with than the little crowd she'd been expecting.

With other people in the room, it would have been easy to make her quick excuses and just pass on through. And she could pretty much count on the fact that nobody would be impolite enough to say something even if she did look a little upset.

But her mother was impossible to fool. And when she was worried about one of her children, there was nothing that had ever stopped her from speaking her mind about it.

Beth tried to duck her head as her mother turned around to see who had just come in. And then she tried to smile to cover her distress.

The result of both of these must have been so strange that her mother's expression changed instantly from mild interest to concern.

"Honey," she said. "What's wrong?"

Beth shook her head, as if that could shake her thoughts—or even the memories of the past hour or so—right out of it.

What was the right thing to do here? she wondered. Part of her wanted desperately to grab her mother and hug her, just like she would have done when she was a little girl. But part of her knew that she was now a grown woman. She didn't want to upset her mother. But even more than that, she didn't want to act like a child when she should act like an adult. She'd never had to treat anyone else's family like her own before. When she and Tom got married, Gloria would be in her life, for life, as well. So what would the consequences be, of telling her mother why she was upset? Did she want her mother going into this wedding holding a grudge against Gloria? Was it something she should keep to herself, to keep the peace in the family?

Stymied, Beth just shut the door behind herself, kicked off her wet shoes on the mat, and leaned back against the counter, folding her arms across her belly.

Her mother gave her a long look. Then she came over and

put her arm around Beth's shoulders. She leaned her head over so that it brushed against Beth's cheek.

"I know you wanted to have this wedding in New York, honey," she said. "I'm sorry if this isn't what you wanted."

Tears sprang to Beth's eyes. An hour ago, she realized, she had thought having her dream wedding in one state or another was the big problem. If only her problems seemed as small as that now.

But when her mother saw the tears in her eyes, she took that as confirmation that she was right.

"I'm just so grateful you came home," she said. "I want you to know how much it means to me. I know your dad's been gone for years, but especially now, with you getting married, it means so much to be doing it in places that he knew, in places that he loved. Even if he can't be here, he *was* here. And that makes all the difference for me. Sometimes I feel like maybe he's just in the next room, you know?"

Beth nodded. She knew exactly what her mother meant. In fact, she'd had the same feeling herself, several times, since she got home. But it wasn't a lonely, haunted feeling. It was more comforting—just the way it always had been when he really was in the next room.

Her mother gave her a squeeze. "I loved your dad so much," she said. "And we were so happy here. And I know that you and Tom are going to be happy, just like we were."

At this, the tears that had simply been leaking from the corners of Beth's eyes up until now began to run down her face in earnest. She desperately wanted to believe that her mother was right. And until this afternoon, she had believed it absolutely. There was no way she would have been marrying Tom if she had any serious questions about that.

But now the distance between her marriage to Tom and her parents' marriage to each other seemed so vast it was hard to see how anyone could ever think they were the same thing. Her parents had been high school sweethearts who had grown up in Blue Hill and known each other all their lives. When they got married, there was a good chance that neither of them had ever heard the word "prenuptial." And Beth could imagine that Mitzi might have given Beth's father a good talking-to before she let him marry her daughter. But she couldn't imagine her grandmother ever saying the kinds of things Gloria had just said to her.

It made her wonder whether her sense that she really knew Tom was just an illusion. And even if she did know him well, it made her wonder if they might just be so different that their marriage could never work, no matter how pretty the wedding was.

"Oh, honey," her mother said, giving her a hug. "I'm sorry. I shouldn't have brought your father up."

Beth shook her head, hugging her mother back. "That's not it," she said, her voice cracking.

Her mother pulled away, wiped the tears from Beth's eyes with her own hands, and looked into Beth's eyes.

"What is it?" she said, her own eyes worried.

There was no point in trying to keep it from her now, Beth realized. If she did, her mother would just worry it was something worse. Not that Beth could think of what that might be, right now.

"It's Gloria," Beth said quietly. "She wants me to sign a prenup."

"A prenup?" her mother said, all the ire that Beth had first felt at the idea flaring up in her eyes. But quickly, she wrestled her own emotions down, to concentrate on her daughter.

Beth nodded.

"What did Tom say?" her mother asked.

"He didn't know," Beth said. "Well, he did. But he told her not to ask me." When she said it this way, aloud, it didn't sound nearly as bad as she had felt when she'd fled and left Tom in the kitchen over at Jen's house.

"What did you tell her?" her mother asked.

"I said no," Beth said.

Her mother gave a fierce little nod. "That's right," she said. Then something like satisfaction lit in her eyes. "What did she say?" she asked, obviously thinking Beth had already won the victory.

Beth's voice cracked as she spoke. "She didn't believe me," Beth said. "She wants to talk again at the rehearsal dinner."

A thundercloud formed on her mother's face. Beth could almost see her mother restraining herself from turning on her heel and marching upstairs to bang on Gloria's door herself. But to Beth's relief, she didn't. Instead, she slid her arm over her daughter's shoulders.

"I don't know what to do," Beth said. "Maybe it doesn't matter. Maybe I should sign it, and just smooth things over. Or maybe if I do, she'll just keep trying to push me around for the rest of my life."

"Why don't you want to sign it?" her mother asked quietly.

When Beth stiffened beside her, her mother gave her a squeeze.

"I'm not saying you should," she said. "I'm asking how you feel."

Beth relaxed back into the warmth of her mother's embrace again. And this time, as she did, her feelings welled up in her: not the shock and anger and denial she'd felt ever since Gloria ambushed her, but the deep hurt and worry under them.

"You know when Prince Harry asked Meghan to marry him?" Beth asked.

"Yes," her mother said, in a tone that made it clear that she didn't know exactly where this was going, but she was game to listen to anything Beth had to say.

"So many people were so jealous of her," Beth said. "But I wasn't."

"Why not?" her mother asked.

"Because everyone was so sure that *she* was the lucky one," Beth said. "That anyone in the world would want to marry him, but that this was the best chance she'd ever have. Nobody ever talked about how lucky he was to get to marry *her*."

"Hm," her mother said, prompting her to go on.

"But it's not easy to marry into a family like that. A life like that," Beth added. "Everyone thinks it must be so perfect, with all the fancy dresses, and parties, and beaches, and clubs. But it's not. And you know what's hardest about it?"

"What?" her mother asked.

"If you're not from there, you—" Beth said, and her voice cracked with emotion. "It's so easy to just get lost. They have all the money, and all the power. Everyone wants to be like them. They think they're doing you a favor just to let you in. And God forbid you don't do exactly what you're supposed to once you're there."

"Like sign a prenup," her mother said.

"Like that," Beth said. "Or a million other things."

She laid her head on her mother's shoulder.

"Why isn't anyone giving *him* a prenup to sign, because he might not be good enough to marry *me*?" Beth asked.

"You want me to?" her mother said quickly. "I can have one ready in ten minutes."

Beth shook her head quickly, but the joke did make her smile. "Thanks, Mom," she said.

"If your dad were here," her mother said, "he'd make sure everyone in that family knew how lucky they are to have you."

"I just hate the way it makes me feel," Beth said. "If we don't start out as equals from the very beginning, then . . ." She trailed off, not sure how to end the sentence. Not sure she wanted to.

Her mother took a deep breath.

"What do you think I should do?" Beth asked.

Her mother let the breath out in a long sigh.

"Oh, honey," she said. "I wish I still had all the answers like I did when you were little. Or like you *thought* I did, anyway," she said, with a slight smile. "But I don't. And I'm not sure anyone else does, either. I think this is one of those places where no one else can tell you what you should do."

She gave Beth another hug, then released her.

"You're going to have to decide what you want," her mother said. "For yourself. I don't know what that is," she added. "But I do know one thing."

"What's that?" Beth said, wiping her eyes.

"I know you can do it," her mother said.

Ten

GLORIA PULLED OPEN THE top drawer of the large bureau that stood opposite the bed in their room, decorated with a surprisingly tasteful golden reindeer, then heaved a sigh.

"What?" Ken asked from behind her, where he had just unzipped his own suitcase.

"It's full," she said, sliding it shut, and opening the one below it. "So is this one."

"Hm," Ken said, hesitating with a pair of socks in his hand.

Gloria, who had two pairs of slacks in her own hand, surveyed the room, but the bureau was the only possible piece of furniture into which they could unpack. She tried the very bottom drawer. This one was full of what looked to be tins of cookies and glass jars. But the jars, instead of being full of jam or something that actually belonged in a jar, were full of buttons and pins.

"There's room in the closet," Ken said, rattling a few garments in plastic bags that hung on the otherwise bare rack.

Gloria pulled the dresses she planned to wear at the rehearsal and wedding from their folding bags and situated them in the closet. But that still left everything else in her bags. And she couldn't very well hang up her underthings, or her sweaters. Or her jewelry or cosmetics.

"Maybe if we think of it as camping," she said, settling her gold cosmetics bag on a nearby shelf, which was stuffed, not with books, but with fabric, as the two top drawers of the bureau had been.

"If we were in Vermont, they'd be charging us double the rates at the Plaza for this," Ken said wryly. "This kind of country charm goes for an arm and a leg."

Gloria found a low table in the corner, which was not really the right size for a luggage stand but would have to work. She settled a bag onto it and opened it up so that she could get to her things without having to scrabble around on the floor—or leave her bag on the bed.

"What's this?" Ken asked.

When she turned around, he was pointing to a small plastic machine built into a desk. He leaned down and peered at the workings: a large round dial at one end, and a cluster of metal work at the other.

"It's a sewing machine, Ken," Gloria said impatiently.

Ken had come from generations of money, but she hadn't. She'd grown up scrabbling in a factory town in Pennsylvania where she'd had to use a sewing machine to make her own dresses, because she couldn't afford any of the ones they had in the stores downtown—which while she was growing up were all closing down, because of the mall they'd built out near Pitts-burgh, even though it was such a long drive you could only really get there on the weekends. It never ceased to amaze her, even decades after they'd married, the things he didn't know. And these days, it never ceased to irritate her.

"A sewing machine?" Ken repeated, bending over to peer into the workings of the needle and foot.

"Haven't you ever seen a sewing machine before?" Gloria asked.

"It doesn't look like the ones at my tailor's," Ken said, by way of explanation.

But this only added to Gloria's irritation. Of course the only sewing machine he'd ever see was at a tailor's.

"This must be Nadine's quilting nook," Gloria said. "That would explain the piles of scraps she's got filling up the bureau."

"They use the scraps, right?" Ken said, putting the pieces together in his mind as if he were making some kind of quilt there himself. "To make the quilt."

Gloria nodded, lifting another bag off the bed to set it down on the floor.

As she did, the papers of the prenup she had dropped there when Beth left the room rustled.

"What's that?" Ken asked.

Gloria hesitated. She hadn't wanted him to see it, but she couldn't bring herself to lie to him. No matter how bad things got between them, they'd always told each other the truth. At least she'd told him. Maybe she'd told him a bit too much—too many of the things that bothered her, too much of her frustrations and disappointments. But in any case, she wasn't going to lie to him now.

"It's that agreement I was telling you about," she said.

For all his faults, Ken wasn't a dumb man. As soon as she said it, she could see the pieces come together in his head. "You asked Beth to sign it," he said, a look of mild horror on his face.

Gloria gave a defiant nod.

"But we talked about it," Ken said. "We agreed. Tom told you no, so you weren't going to—"

He wasn't telling her anything she didn't already know. So as usual, she got straight to the point. "Well," she said, "I did."

Now Ken was angry. "I never thought this was a good idea in the first place," he said. "I told you we should stay out of it. I was willing to have you draw up the papers, since you felt so strongly about it. But this is something else, now. What did Beth say?"

"I'm going to talk with her again at the rehearsal dinner," Gloria said smoothly. When Ken was calm, he often drove her crazy. But when he was upset, she actually got a kind of devilish pleasure in staying calm, at least on the surface.

"Gloria!" Ken said. "You can't do that. She already told you no, didn't she?"

In reply, Gloria gave a curt nod.

Ken shook his head. "You're pushing too hard," he said. "Tom doesn't want this. Beth doesn't want it. And this is the night before their wedding. You're in danger of ruining this memory for them."

"They don't know what they want!" Gloria burst out, stung by his words. "They're just kids. They have no idea what a marriage is really going to be like, for all those years."

Ken just looked at her, for a long moment. Then he said, "Like we didn't?"

Gloria almost snapped back, "That's not what I meant." But then she realized, maybe she did.

The thought was too hard to bear, so she turned back to the track of her earlier argument. "You seem to think I'm out to ruin this wedding," she said. "But it's exactly the opposite. This is about Tom's happiness. I'm just trying to protect him. This is the only way he can know for sure what she's really after. If she really loves him, only him, why should the money matter to her? Why didn't she just sign it?"

"You didn't sign any agreement," Ken said. "When we got married."

Against her will, his comment pulled her back to the days of her wedding—thoughts she'd been trying to push down ever since Tom and Beth had announced their engagement. It wasn't because the memories were so painful that she didn't want to bring them up again. It was because they were so good. She and

Ken had been so in love back then, so sure of each other and what they wanted. She had no idea how they had gotten to here from there. It was easier never to think about it.

But now she couldn't help it. Her mind flashed to one of her favorite memories: the way Ken scooped her up when they stepped out of the church and carried her down the giant stone steps, in a huge flurry of confetti from their assembled guests. It wasn't the pageantry of it all that stayed with her. It was how safe she had felt at that moment, and the way that, even with all those people and all that hoopla around them, it had felt as if they were the only two people in the world.

The memory of it brought tears to her eyes.

Ken, whose jaw had been set and ready for more fight, suddenly looked stricken when he saw them.

"Gloria," he said, coming around to the side of the bed where she was standing to put his arm around her shoulders. "I'm sorry."

Gloria almost asked, *For what?* For all the times he'd left her alone during the past years, roaming off to business deals all over the world without her, or working until all hours even when he was in the city? For never noticing all the things she tried to do to make the houses, or herself, so special that he'd want to stay there longer—even just a few minutes more? For clamming up and turning away when she got angry, instead of being there with her, even if it was just to have an argument?

But suddenly, she was so tired. And even with all the water that had passed under the bridge between them, she still longed for the feel of his arm around her, and still felt an echo of that sense of safety she had felt on the first day they were married— even if that echo was faint.

She swayed against him, and his grip around her tightened.

"It's going to be all right," he said, his voice soothing. "You can just see they're going to be happy."

Years ago, Gloria had loved the way that Ken was always able to look on the bright side. But now she'd started to wonder if it was just his way of hiding from the truth—or refusing to see it at all. Things didn't always turn out for the best, the way Ken was always predicting they would. Bad things did happen. And if you were busy pretending that bad things never happened, you couldn't watch out and protect yourself and the people you loved.

"You can't really think they don't love each other," Tom said. "I mean, look at the two of them."

"I know they do," Gloria admitted. "But sometimes that's not enough. Things don't always turn out the way we hope they will."

Ken was quiet for a long moment, gently supporting her as she leaned into him. Then he asked, "Did we not turn out the way you hoped?"

The twist in Gloria's heart at this question was so deep that if he hadn't been holding on to her, she might actually have reeled on her feet. But just as soon as the wave of emotion rolled over her, she slammed some door shut in her heart, leaving all of that on the other side.

It wasn't that she couldn't bear to think about it, she told herself.

What did it matter what she thought about that or not? They'd been living the way they had, almost as strangers, for years now. What could either of them do about it after all this time?

Ken always thought things might get better. But he didn't know. If they tried to drag all of this out in the open now, after so long, it might very well get worse.

It was practically a nonsense question, she told herself.

That was why she couldn't bring herself to answer.

Eleven

JEN DROVE UP THE winding drive that led to the Deans' house with a sense of relief—not just that they'd made it back safely in the midst of the brewing storm, which had already dumped a good inch of snow on the surrounding hills and fields while she was gone, but that she could finally get out of the car with Jared.

A few minutes after they'd lapsed into silence over his comments about Ed, Jared had just started up again, as if nothing had happened. And he didn't just act like they hadn't just had a little spat in the car. He acted as if he'd never left.

Well, not exactly. Before, when they were together, he would have had her hand firmly in his if the two of them were anywhere in reach. And he didn't make any move to do anything like that now. But he talked with the same easy familiarity they'd always had between them, making jokes about the other drivers, telling her little facts about his life, bantering back and forth with her whenever she'd give him anything to work with at all. Just as if he had no memory of the fact that he'd been off in Texas for the last three years, without her.

And the problem was, Jen couldn't help feeling as if he'd never left, too. It was amazing: just by walking back into her life, Jared had made it seem as if the past three years hadn't really happened, or were only some kind of long dream. She fell just as easily as he did into all their old familiar patterns, their inside jokes, all the things they already knew about each other.

Try as she might, she couldn't conjure up the hurt or anger she wanted to feel. She'd been plenty hurt when he left, but she'd had enough time now for that hurt to seem faint, especially when Jared was sitting right there beside her, prattling away. And she'd been plenty angry, but she'd never really been sure about what. Jared had never lied to her. He'd never made her any promises he didn't keep. He'd never cheated on her, or said anything to run her down or demean her or make her small. When she heard the stories from other girls of other things guys had done to them, she never really felt like she could jump in, because what had he done that was really so bad?

At heart, she'd only ever been hurt and angry because she simply wanted him to come back. And now that he was here, she didn't even feel happy. It was even worse than that. She felt as if somehow the whole world had settled back into place, as if she'd been walking around for years with her shoes on the wrong feet, and had finally just switched them back.

It was as confusing as anything that had ever happened to her. Maybe, she tried to tell herself, it was just because they'd known each other for so long—as long as either of them could remember, since they'd grown up next door from the time they were tiny. Once, when they were in high school, they'd tried to figure out what their earliest memories of each other were. Jen remembered that Jared had climbed up on a chicken coop when he was somewhere under three, with a feather he'd gotten from the coop, insisting that now he could fly, just like Dumbo in the movie. And Jared's first memory of her had been when he came over as a toddler and she'd spent all afternoon making him pretend that she was the trail boss on a westward pioneer expedition, and he was her donkey.

Of course, she reasoned, with a history that went back that far, she couldn't help but feel comfortable around him. He was practically like family—even if he never really would be now, the way they'd sometimes dreamed.

But in the back of her mind, something whispered that it might not be just that. There were lots of other people in town whom she'd known for just as long as Jared. Even people who she'd played with from such a young age. Including Ed, whose mom had recently shown her a picture she took of the two of them when they were on the same T-ball team, as four-year-olds. That was just the way life was in a small town. And none of them made her feel the way she felt seeing Jared again now, after so long.

She couldn't seem to do anything about it. So she couldn't wait to get away from Jared, so that she could clear her head and get her internal balance again.

She figured she could make it until she got to the top of her father's drive, when she'd run over to see what was happening with the preparations for the rehearsal dinner. Because she and Jared were so late getting back, the rehearsal itself was already in full swing, if it was going as scheduled. She should have been there for it, but it was more important that the brother of the bride not miss the wedding. And now it was more important that she make sure everything was all right with the rehearsal dinner than that she pick up the last few minutes of the rehearsal itself. Despite all the fuss made over it, the rehearsal for the wedding was really one of the least important details. One way or another, everyone would make it down the aisle, and usually dressed and in the correct order. But if the food wasn't ready when the hungry guests showed, up, God help them all.

In the meantime, she guessed, Jared would head over to find

out what he'd missed at the rehearsal—or just take his things over to Beth's place to stay in his old room.

"Okay," she said when she took the keys out of the ignition. "I'll see you at dinner."

She hopped out of the car and started off for the Deans' small barn, where the party was hopefully coming together even as they spoke. But when she did, she realized that Jared was following her.

She stopped. "Don't you need to get your bag?" she said.

Jared shook his head cheerfully. "I'll grab it on the way back," he said. "I just want to see what magic you've put together in the barn. The last time I saw it, it was full of straw and lumber and old tractor parts."

This happened to be a very accurate inventory of the barn's former contents, as Jen knew from the huge cleanup effort she'd had to undertake and oversee in order to get the place into any shape that guests might actually enjoy.

But that didn't mean she wanted Jared trailing after her like a puppy.

"You're not cold?" she asked, in a last-ditch effort to get him to go inside and leave her in peace.

Jared grinned. "Little lady," he said, diving into a drawl she'd never heard before, which she suspected he'd picked up in Texas, "I may have been living in Dallas for the past few years. But I'm *from* Michigan."

Jen shook her head in hopes of shaking off the delight she felt at the sight of his grin. When it wouldn't shake, she simply turned on her heel and headed off for the Dean barn. No matter how Jared had her rattled, she couldn't let it affect the wedding. And it had been well over an hour since she'd seen what was happening with the dinner prep. All the wedding planning books she'd read had emphasized the importance of having your planner on hand for those crucial last moments before an event. She hated that she'd been away so long already. And nothing could have persuaded her to do it, if it hadn't been for the fact that if she hadn't made the trip to the airport, the bride's brother might have missed the rehearsal dinner.

Jared tramped along behind her, in the little fleece vest that apparently passed for foul-weather gear down in Texas, humming a scrap of some Christmas song that he'd probably heard the tune of over the PA system at the airport or on the plane, without even knowing how it wound up in his mind.

When she got to the doors of the barn, for the first time since she'd picked him up, all thoughts of Jared finally flew her mind. The question of what the barn would look like beyond those doors was simply too big for anything else to compete with. All the guests who were streaming into town tonight, from all over the country, all those strangers and friends: What were they going to see when they first walked in the door, at the very first event for the very first wedding she had ever planned?

Then she took a breath, slid the big bolt that held the two large barn doors together aside to release it, and looked in.

She and Jared gasped almost in unison.

Jen had had dreams about what the place would look like, made drawings, and had what seemed like endless discussions with the caterers and florists and the suppliers who sent her the big paper lanterns that were the visual touchstone of the night's decorations. But this was better than she'd even imagined.

The Deans' barn was smaller than hers, about half the size. Because they hadn't ever had as much livestock as the Fitzgeralds, it didn't have the same warren of stalls and bins that Jen's family barn had on the ground floor, which also had a cement block, just like Jen's family's. But the Dean barn had something in some ways even more magical: a beautiful second-floor hayloft that floated over the entire bottom floor of the barn, with slatted wooden stairs that led up to the vast room under the peak of the roof, with several large windows that Beth's father had installed himself, not because there was any particular agricultural call for them, but simply because he liked the light.

The floor of the loft had been neatly covered with large vintage rugs that she'd collected in thrift stores all over the region, including a set of runners that ran from the door to the serving area, where two long tables were set up, in order to accommodate all the out-of-town guests. Large white paper lanterns hung from the beams of the loft, casting light down on the tables below, but also giving a beautiful underlighting to the peak of the barn roof above. Even from the foot of the stairs to the loft, which led up to the left of the main barn doors, Jen could see the glitter of glasses and silver on the tables, and the green sprigs of the runners of greenery that ran down the length of each table.

Quietly, as if she might scare all the magic away if she took a step that was just a little bit too loud, she mounted the steps, Jared behind her.

"Wow," he said when they stepped out into the loft itself, where caterers were still busily laying out napkins and setting down pats of butter on small round plates. "This is amazing."

"Thanks," Jen said.

To their right, there was a stack of soda cases: not just the usual suspects, but locally sourced sodas, and a few old favorites, piled up near a table that was clearly set to become the bar.

As soon as he saw the cases, Jared went straight for the top one: Cherry Coke, which had been a favorite drink of both of theirs from the time they were kids.

"Okay if I take one of these, boss?" he asked with a grin. "For old times' sake?"

Jen nodded.

Jared swiped a bottle opener from the bar tools, popped the top, took a sip, and wrinkled his nose. "Could use some ice," he said.

"There are glasses right there," Jen said, pointing.

Jared collected a glass from the dozens that were neatly lined on the table, awaiting the guests, and looked around the table. Then he lifted up the white skirt of the cloth and looked underneath.

"Where's the ice?" he asked.

"Heidi," Jen said, catching the eye of the caterer, who was going by with a tray full of small glass salt and pepper shakers. "Where's the ice?"

"It's by the bar," Heidi said.

Jen shook her head.

Heidi's eyebrows drew together. "Ben!" she yelled.

A skinny high school kid with a blue bandana tied around his head came scampering up.

"Where's the ice?" Heidi asked him.

The speed with which his expression turned from willingness to horror made it clear that some kind of mistake had been made.

"I'll go get some," he said. "I'll get some right away."

"You can't go now," Heidi said. "It's going to be everything we can do to get this dinner on as it is."

Jen's mind began to click, trying to figure out if she could make yet another trip. But the guests were supposed to arrive for the dinner in less than an hour, and she was still wearing a flannel shirt and a pair of red leggings. She didn't see any way she could make it work.

"I'll do it," Jared said. "Give me your keys."

Jen reached for her keys, but as she did, she began to protest. "I don't know if you—"

Jared plucked the keys from her hand. "How many pounds do you need?" he asked.

"At least fifty," Heidi said.

"*Whoosh!*" Jared said. "You can't just pack that soda in some snow?"

But he was already heading for the door. And before Heidi could shoot an answer back, he'd disappeared.

Heidi looked after him with clear admiration. But Jen, who had been so eager to get rid of him, now sighed in exasperation. She'd thought she would feel better if she could just get him to go away. But now that she had, she missed him. Wasn't there some kind of button she could push that would make her stop feeling anything about him?

As she wondered this, the door of the barn swung open.

She looked up in expectation, annoyed at how glad she was at the prospect of seeing Jared again, even though he'd just left— and wondering what else in the world could have gone wrong. Had her car chosen just this moment to break down?

"Hey, babe," Ed said.

He was as handsome as always, his dark hair slicked back, wearing a gingham shirt and a dark suit coat, a pair of jeans, and his best pair of cowboy boots. "It looks real pretty in here," he said.

With a surge of relief, Jen went over and gave him a kiss, hoping it would drive the memory of Jared right out of her mind.

For a moment, it did.

"I'm so proud of you, baby," he said, when he released her. "I knew you could do it. I don't think I've ever seen anything that looked so nice."

Jen's heart warmed for a minute, until her mind kicked in, with something that sounded suspiciously like Jared's voice, to remind her of how little of the world Ed had actually seen.

"I brought you something," Ed said.

"Oh?" Jen asked.

Ed nodded, his eyes shining.

Jen glanced around, trying not to feel impatient. It was so sweet he had thought to bring her something, but she could use twice as much time as she had, and this was taking up what time she did have.

And then he produced a box that was at least a foot by a foot square. Jen couldn't figure out where the heck he had been hiding it, but apparently he'd just had it stashed on some nearby chair.

When she opened it and pulled it out, she couldn't figure out what it was at first: just a big round tube of glass, bent in at both ends, but open on both ends as well, so it wouldn't even work as a vase.

"Oh," she said. "Wow."

"You like it?" Ed asked eagerly. "It's one of those hurricane lamps, like you liked at the restaurant the other night. I saw one in an antique barn, and I thought, *I'll just get that for her, so she can have one of her own.*"

Jen smiled. It was just like Ed—always observing what she liked.

But also, she had no need whatsoever for a hurricane lantern in the midst of this rehearsal dinner.

She gave him a quick kiss. "Um," she said. "It's so nice. I don't want to break it. Do you think you can take it for me?"

"Yeah?" Ed said, obviously disappointed that she wasn't setting it up to gaze at right that instant.

"Just till all this"—Jen said, gesturing at the growing hullaballoo around them—"is over."

"Oh," Ed said, somewhat crestfallen as he retrieved the box. "Sure."

"Thanks, sweetie," Jen said. "I mean it."

"Hey," Ed said, as she started to turn away, to handle whatever crazy thing might come next, "I saw Jared in the yard. What's he doing here?"

She could tell from his tone of voice that he hadn't been happy to see her old flame.

"He went to get some ice," Jen said. Then she felt guilty, as if she had just told some kind of lie. And then she felt aggravated that thoughts of Jared made her feel guilty, when she knew for a fact she hadn't done anything wrong. And aggravated with Ed, for maybe no reason at all.

"It's not like we could have the wedding without him," she said, wishing with all her heart that they could have. "He's the brother of the bride."

Twelve

DESTINY GAZED INTO THE mirror in her bedroom, put on a swipe of bright lipstick, and then gazed at her reflection.

To her surprise, she liked what she saw.

She'd been fighting to finish her bridesmaid's dress all afternoon, and as she'd started to try it on, she'd realized that it was never going to look especially flattering on her, no matter how well she sewed it. Resigned, she'd told herself that was the way of all bridesmaids' dresses, although she still wasn't thrilled with the idea of showing up in front of all Beth's fancy New York friends in something other than her best.

But tonight, she was wearing the dress she'd bought for herself, for the rehearsal dinner, a simple black sheath with a folded neckline that gave it just a bit of edge, which she hoped would give the clear message that not everyone in Blue Hill was as unsophisticated as the city folk might think.

It skimmed her figure in all the right ways, and her curly auburn hair, which lived somewhere between unruly and impossible nine days out of ten, had decided to choose this night to be absolutely perfect, waving back off her face in the two jeweled barrettes she'd swept it back in almost as if she was some movie star from the glamour days of the old black-and-white films.

It was the first time she'd really liked how she looked in a long time. And she was grateful it had happened tonight, of all nights.

"Mommy, Mommy, Mommy, Mommy!" Cody bellowed behind the door. As she turned away from the mirror, slipping the lipstick into her beaded clutch, he came barreling through the door, his red clip-on tie askew, one sock on, and one foot bare.

But when he saw her, he came to a dead stop, even losing interest momentarily in the piece of bread spread with peanut butter that Destiny approvingly noticed Carl had apparently given him. That was ninja-level parenting on Carl's part—the rehearsal dinner wasn't scheduled to begin until seven thirty, which in kid food time might as well be midnight—and there was no guarantee it would really start on time.

Then Jessie appeared in the door behind Cody, in the turquoise tulle dress she'd insisted on wearing that night.

"Mommy!" she breathed. "You're so beautiful!"

It crossed Destiny's mind that the surprise in her daughter's tone was something of a backhanded compliment, but she felt so good that she just let it go, crouching down to give them both a quick hug.

That's when she felt it: the slap of something quite a bit larger than Cody's little hand on her hip, as he reached up to squeeze her back.

"Cody," she said in a warning tone, but it was already too late.

At the change in her tone of voice, both her kids backed up cautiously, so she had an absolutely clear view of the piece of bread with peanut butter that was now attached to her hip.

Which was the moment Carl chose to come through the door, a grin of victory on his face, holding up a single sock.

"One more sock to go!" he crowed. "And then all the Bard kids will be dressed!"

This was, in fact, a genuine accomplishment. Jessie knew how to dress herself, but could never decide on a single outfit, so even when she was fully dressed, it was always an open question of how long it would last before she was back in her room, trying something else on, often at the very least opportune moment. And Cody was an escape artist when it came to clothes, which he still thought of mainly as instruments of torture, to be discarded as quickly as possible.

But as Destiny's stomach dropped, realizing her dress for the night had just been ruined, she was in no mood to celebrate with Carl.

"Couldn't you keep them out of here for even five minutes?" she asked, yanking the piece of bread off her hip. Just as she'd feared, there was still a giant spot of sticky peanut butter.

"What in the . . . ?" Carl began.

"It's Cody's," Destiny said, throwing the bread in the trash can beside her mirror.

She thought she saw the faintest smile twitch over Carl's lips as he took in the situation, but he knew better than to vent his amusement, if that's what it really was. Instead, he grabbed each kid by one hand and started to back out of the room.

"We're almost ready," he said, in his most calming voice.

"Well," Destiny said, her own high with emotion, "I'm not!"

Somehow, the four of them managed to get to the Fitzgerald barn, where the rehearsal was to be held, at something approximating the right time.

"I'll be over here," Carl said, shuffling the kids toward a group of chairs that had been occupied by people who were clearly not part of the wedding party itself. "With the other non-essentials." He gave her a grin and a wink, then kissed her cheek.

Destiny took a deep breath, and started down toward the little knot of the wedding party.

When she got there, Beth and Tom were deep in conversation with the minister over some detail of the program. She tried to catch Beth's eye, but Beth barely smiled at her before looking back at Tom.

You could never expect much of a bride's attention at her wedding, Destiny told herself. But still, it stung. There had been a time in their life when both of them would have dropped anything at the sight of the other one. But so many other things got in the way now. And maybe, Destiny realized, Beth had actually felt the same way about Destiny, first. There had been so many times she'd been too busy to call Beth, because she was dealing with Carl or the kids.

"You must be Destiny," someone said behind her.

Destiny turned to see a tall woman, about her age, dressed all in black, with perfectly blown-out, stick-straight blond hair, and a big smile.

"I'm Sylvia," the woman said, sticking her hand out.

"Oh," Destiny said, suddenly nervous to find herself face-to-face with one of the actual New York people. When she hadn't really known what any of them were like, it had been easy to think of them as the kind of plastic characters she was used to seeing on TV. But looking into Sylvia's eyes was more confusing. There was no question that Sylvia was intimidating, with her perfect hair and clothes. But when she was standing right there, it was impossible not to see that Sylvia was also just a regular person, like Destiny, or anybody.

"Are you the other bridesmaid?" Destiny asked.

Sylvia grimaced and nodded. "I thought I was going to get away with only doing this once in my life," she said. "For my cousin Lydia, when I was nineteen." She grinned. "I always swore the only way I'd be a bridesmaid again was at a destination wedding. When Beth asked me to come to Michigan in the middle of winter, I told her I guessed I should have been more specific in what I meant by 'destination.'"

She laughed at her own joke, but Destiny didn't join her. What was the joke supposed to be? Destiny wondered. That her hometown was some kind of a punch line?

But Sylvia didn't seem to notice whether Destiny had laughed or not. She glanced at Destiny's dress, paying especially close attention to the scarf Destiny had tied around the silhouette of the sheath, hoping to cover the remaining evidence of the peanut butter, since she didn't have anything else that was even remotely presentable for the rehearsal dinner.

"That's an interesting scarf," Sylvia said. "I've never seen anyone tie it quite that way. Is that something people do around here?"

Destiny could tell that Sylvia wasn't trying to cut her down—not on purpose. But the way Sylvia asked her question made her feel like an animal in the zoo. And one who had put her stripes on wrong, not nearly as chic as the other animals in the fancier zoo downtown. It wasn't a nice feeling.

"Um . . ." Destiny began.

Before she could answer, Jen swooped in and caught her by the elbow. "Sylvia!" she said. "So nice to see you."

Sylvia grinned at her. "I didn't know if we were gonna make it," she said. "I've been in a lot of airport shuttles before, but none quite like this one."

Destiny wasn't sure how Sylvia had managed to do it, but she could tell by the look on Jen's face that Sylvia had just taken the wind out of Jen's sails, just the way she'd taken them out of Destiny's.

"It wasn't exactly the original plan," Jen said, looking abashed.

"Well," Sylvia said cheerfully, "I can't imagine what the original plan must have been!"

"Can I talk to you for a minute?" Jen asked Destiny.

With relief, Destiny nodded. She and Jen both did their best to paste sincere-looking smiles on their faces as they left Sylvia behind, and Jen pulled Destiny over into a corner.

"Can you do me a favor?" Jen asked.

"Does it involve Sylvia?" Destiny asked.

Jen shook her head and the two of them exchanged a meaningful glance.

"It's about the rehearsal dinner," Jen said. "You're seated at a table with a lot of family."

"Oh," Destiny said, her heart warming. It was nice to know Beth was keeping her that close.

"Including Tom's uncle Charlie," Jen said. The look she gave when she said his name said everything Destiny needed to know. Apparently, Uncle Charlie was considered some kind of black sheep of the family. Destiny raised her eyebrows.

"Is there anything in particular I should know?" Destiny asked.

"Can you just"—Jen said, hesitating as she searched for the right words—"keep an eye on him?"

"Oh!" Destiny said, feeling a little let down. "Oh, sure."

"You're the best," Jen said in a rush. Then she squeezed Destiny's hand and disappeared into the crowd again.

Destiny sighed. She tried not to feel a little sad that Beth hadn't just asked her herself. And that the job she'd been given was so small in the grand scheme of the wedding. She wanted Beth to know she was really there for her on these important days. That was the point of being a bridesmaid: not just putting the dress on and standing up in front of everyone. She would have been willing to do something that mattered a lot more, even if it meant more work.

After all, she thought, how bad could this uncle Charlie really be?

Thirteen

"YOU SURE GOT THIS old barn done up nice," Mitzi cracked as the laugh lines crinkled around her eyes. "It looks so good I'm about to see if I can get someone to build me a Jacuzzi out in the chicken coop."

Mitzi's glance, as always, was wry. But Beth could see the joy in her grandmother's eyes as she took Beth's palm in her own timeworn hands and pressed it warmly. Beth knew her grandmother wasn't one for big displays of affection, but at the clear sight of the love and pride in her grandmother's eyes, she couldn't help herself. She leaned over and enveloped Mitzi in a big hug.

"All right, all right," Mitzi began to protest after about half a second, squirming to get out of her grasp like an energetic kid. "I'm not the only one here, you know. All those others folks are lined up to see you, too."

She nodded back at the cluster of guests who had started to knot up behind her, just inside the loft, waiting to greet Beth and Tom before they went to sit down.

With one last squeeze, Beth released Mitzi, who made a big show of straightening her dress.

"Has this woman been bothering you?" Tom asked, in a joking tone, giving Beth a glance of mock censure.

"Oh, I don't know that I'd say that," Mitzi said, grinning.

She always tried to keep from letting her emotions go with her family, but she couldn't hide her total adoration of Tom. From the first time she'd met him, she'd lit up like a schoolgirl around him. In her eyes, he could do absolutely no wrong.

"You'll let me know, though?" Tom went on. "If anyone gives you any trouble?"

Mitzi gave a definitive nod, still trying to move along to let the other guests give their greetings, too.

But Tom shook his head.

"I'm afraid there's just one other thing I'll have to ask you for, though," he said seriously.

"Oh?" Mitzi said, leaning in gamely, with none of her usual suspicion or reserve.

Before she could object, Tom gathered her up into a gigantic bear hug of his own that actually lifted her feet a few inches off the ground.

"Tom Allerton!" Mitzi objected, her voice full of delight. "You put me down!"

Tom obeyed, then planted a kiss on Mitzi's cheek before she was able to dart away.

It was exactly the kind of thing that Beth had always loved about Tom—his easy way with all people, including the ones who didn't always make it easy. And as Mitzi stepped away, Tom looked back at her, his eyes full of laughter, as he did so often. Beth loved these private moments between the two of them, too. Even surrounded by a crowd, as they were now, he always made her feel like she was the most important thing in the world.

But now, moments after their eyes met, Tom's gaze slid away from hers, as if he was afraid to look too long, because of what he might see if he did.

Beth had never seen him do this before, in all the time they'd spent together, and the sight of it made her feel dizzy.

She understood why he might not want to look too long. They hadn't talked, not really, since she had stalked out of the kitchen, ending their conversation about the prenup his mother wanted her to sign. He'd given her a kiss when they arrived at the Fitzgerald barn for the rehearsal, and told her how beautiful she looked in her dress, a dove-gray velvet sheath which she was wearing with a brooch her mother had given her—and a pair of high-water rain boots, suitable for tromping through the snow.

The whole wedding party had laughed together about the ridiculous getup, and Tom and Beth had laughed with them. And of course, he'd helped her when she changed into the jeweled heels she had waiting for her in the loft, where the rehearsal dinner was laid out.

But there had been so much going on since they last spoke that Beth hadn't even had the chance to think about how she felt about the prenup—let alone how to express whatever she felt to Tom.

And the last thing he had heard, she'd been mad enough to walk out of a conversation—something she'd never done before. It was no wonder he was feeling leery of looking into her eyes too long—even if it was the night before their wedding. Or maybe, especially because it was.

Before she could sort any of that out, Beth felt a hand on her forearm. When she turned to look, it turned into a hug—from Destiny.

"Oh my gosh," Beth said, pulling away to look at Destiny's dress. "That's beautiful. Or, *you're* beautiful, I should say. Thank you so much for being here."

Destiny smiled as Carl reached out to hug Beth as well.

"Welcome home, kid," Carl said, thumping Beth thoroughly on the back.

"And you remember Tom," Beth said, as Tom stuck out his hand to pump Carl's, and both men grinned. They'd spent an afternoon together the past summer, when Beth brought Tom out to meet her family, and it turned out the two of them were both serious trivia nerds.

"Where are the kids?" Beth asked, looking around.

"Jen collected them at the door!" Destiny said, beaming. "She hired a couple of sitters, and they're taking care of them over in their own little play area."

Beth glanced over. Jen had set up the children at special kid-sized tables, with toys for the little ones, and drawings and games for the ones who were a bit older. A column of iridescent soap bubbles was rising from the spot, from what appeared to be a small armory of soap-bubble guns.

"Look how pretty that is," Tom said, following her gaze up to the rafters, where the soap bubbles drifted lazily among the exposed beams.

His hand just touched the back of her dress as he said it, as it had a hundred times before, while he'd pointed out a hundred other things. At the feel of it, Beth felt a rush of love and security, just as she always did. But then something about his touch changed. His hand fluttered at her waist, then pulled away as Destiny and Carl drifted past them, looking for their seats at the long tables filled with flowers and lush table settings, plates of butter and thick chunks of white farm bread.

Startled by the change in Tom, Beth turned to see Ken and Gloria, whose wide smile looked to her like the grin of a shark that had just come face-to-face with an especially delicious fish.

"Mom," Tom said, and wrapped her in a warm hug.

When Gloria reached up to hug him back, Beth could see her face turn on his shoulder and her eyes close in happiness. The expression on her face was so different, and so peaceful, that she almost looked like a child.

Beth was so startled by the change that she looked at Ken. But when she did, he glanced away quickly, almost the same way Tom had just moments before. Had Tom learned that habit from his dad? Beth wondered, with a twist in her heart. And had Ken learned it because Gloria could be so hard to deal with? Or was Gloria so hard to deal with because Ken wasn't ever really fully there?

Before she could even begin to think about any of this, Tom released Gloria and reached out to embrace his dad, leaving Gloria and Beth standing face-to-face.

It was all Beth could do not to recoil from Gloria, which she wanted to do with every fiber of her being. But instead, she opened her arms.

The gesture seemed to freeze Gloria in place. It was as if she hadn't considered, until this very moment, that she might actually be required to hug Beth in the receiving line, and not just her own son. But after a few moments, something seemed to kick in in her mind, reminding her how it would look to refuse Beth's hug in front of all those people.

Gloria shuffled forward, gave Beth a quick squeeze, then stepped back as if she was afraid she might catch something if she stayed too close to Beth for too long.

Then Ken darted in to give her his own brief hug, never meeting her eyes.

"Love you," Tom called after them as they moved on and the next guests stepped up.

Beth reached for his arm, and he folded her hand close to

him, drawing her in. But as she smiled and nodded, greeting one of Tom's good buddies from the city, Beth couldn't calm down the riot of questions in her head. It felt so good to be close to Tom now, as if they'd passed through some kind of storm together. But what if he was just playacting now, for show, like his mom?

She couldn't stop thinking about the way his eyes had turned away from hers, and the way his father's had, too. Was this how it was going to be from now on? Was this how it started, a marriage as cold and stifling as Ken and Gloria's? They must have loved each other when they first got married, or at least thought they did. But look at them now.

Was Gloria right to want her to sign the prenup, absolutely right? Was it possible that Gloria knew something that neither Beth nor Tom were smart enough to recognize yet? Maybe about them, or maybe just about marriage itself? Were they wrong for each other? Was it just too hard to stay in love for a lifetime, even if you found the right one? Were she and Tom destined to turn out like Gloria and Ken?

And was there anything, anything at all, that she could do to stop that?

Fourteen

"SYLVIA," BRADY SCHERMERHORN SAID, pushing through the little crowd that had formed beside the bar to give her a quick, businesslike New York hug. "Thank God you're here."

Sylvia patted him gamely for the half second, but warily. She'd always known Brady was interested in her—despite the fact that she'd never been particularly interested herself, although she'd never been able to put a finger on exactly why. But she did feel a surge of warmth for him now, glad not to be totally alone in a crowd of strangers.

When he released her, she watched as he looked around the barn, and the gathered crowd, with an uneasy expression, as if he had just caught sight of someone walking erratically on the city streets up ahead of him, and wasn't sure yet if it was going to turn out to be someone he'd want to avoid, or just a kid about to break into a dance routine, to ask for tips.

Brady was a perfect example of a classic New York City breed. He was big, strong, smart, handsome, and perfectly dressed—at least, if he'd been in New York—his suit impeccably tailored, his obviously expensive shoes shined to a high gloss on which drops of snow were currently melting into pools, which gave off about the same shine as the leather beneath them. Like Sylvia, he'd been born in the city, gone to city schools, all the way through college, and made his home there now. In his own domain, which stretched from approximately Ninety-Sixth Street to the foot of Manhattan, his instincts were unerring, and his command of any situation was complete.

But take him even half a mile out of his native environment, and he wasn't curious about other ways of life, or things he'd never seen before—because, in his mind, there couldn't be anything worth seeing that wasn't already in New York City. And in response, whenever his feet left his hallowed ground of Manhattan, even if it was only to cross the river to Brooklyn, he began to whine.

The whining was meant to be funny. "I mean," Brady said, "everyone keeps saying how much they fixed up this old barn. As if it never occurred to them you could have a wedding *somewhere other than a barn.*"

When Sylvia smiled, it wasn't because she thought his comment was amusing—she'd never liked his way of cutting down anything he didn't understand. But she'd just come from a conversation with the father of the wedding planner, Mr. Fitzgerald, and the crotchety old farmer had said almost exactly the same thing. The fact that Brady, who considered himself so incredibly sophisticated, was recycling comments that had already been made by someone he'd write off as an old hayseed in a small Michigan town gave her a strong tinge of amusement.

Encouraged by her smile, Brady took a breath, ready to dive in to some further clever side-eye about exactly what he thought about the strange ways of these backward Midwesterners. But before he could, a tall man wearing a black-and-red plaid shirt and a brown corduroy blazer walked up.

"Sylvia," he said matter-of-factly, with a smile.

It was clear to Sylvia that he thought he knew her—which was supported by the fact that he knew her name. But as she looked up at his ruddy face, and the thick blond waves that he'd combed back for the occasion, she couldn't place him as anything other than a rather attractive and strapping version of a young Santa Claus.

"Let me guess," Brady said, sticking out his hand with the aggressive but still somehow cold cordiality of a high-flying New Yorker. "Local boy."

Whoever their new companion was, Sylvia observed, he wasn't stupid. At the slight dig from Brady, his smile clouded to a glower—and immediately Sylvia recognized him.

When she'd first met him, he'd been bundled up in a parka, sporting a several-weeks beard, and hunched grouchily over a steering wheel, which was why she hadn't been able to place him all cleaned up, with a smile on his face. It was Winston, the driver of her pickup van.

Winston looked Brady up and down, pausing for a long beat at Brady's Italian shoes. It was a perfect replication of the way high-class New Yorkers sized one another up, following the old maxim to "look at their shoes"—because a suit could be faked, but good shoes were hard to counterfeit. But Winston, it turned out, had been doing a somewhat different calculation.

"Those the best snow boots they sell in New York?" he asked.

In reply, both Sylvia and Brady looked down at Winston's own feet in unison.

As the foundation of his buffalo-check-and-corduroy-coat look, Sylvia observed, was a pair of Levi's that she suspected had been bought as full-dark denim, and actually worn into their current state of perfect dilapidation, perhaps over the course of a decade. They might even have been, she suspected, Winston's *only* pair of jeans during that decade. But for all the pairs of designer denim she'd seen in her lifetime, paired with everything from crisply pressed oxford shirts to five-hundred-dollar bamboo T-shirts, she'd never seen a pair that looked as right as these.

And his shoes, she told herself, weren't so bad: a good solid pair of work boots, but ones that clearly hadn't seen work yet, just as clearly worn to the upscale gathering as a sign of respect. She'd seen ones just like them the week before at a tony downtown store, already used, marked vintage, and on sale for a thousand bucks a pair, which she strongly suspected was not the original market price of the pair Winston was currently sporting.

They actually did a reasonable job doubling for dress shoes, with a nice shine on the leather, a reasonable round toe—and a good sturdy tread, for traversing the snow that lay everywhere beyond the cozy loft they were currently ensconced in.

When Brady looked back up, speechless, Winston grinned at Sylvia. "So how has Blue Hill been treating you today?" he asked. "We may not have a Starbucks, but I'd say this is a pretty good champagne."

Sylvia raised her eyebrows, surprised. He was right that it was a good champagne. Jen, the planner, clearly knew her stuff—at least well enough to hire a caterer with taste. But she wouldn't exactly have expected Winston to be a champagne aficionado.

"Try not to look so surprised," Winston said wryly. "I've been a champagne man since I stole my first bottle at my sister's wedding, when I was nineteen. And believe it or not, there are one or two good bars outside of New York City."

"There's not a Starbucks here?" Brady repeated, in a tone of alarm. He looked to Sylvia as if he was expecting her to take his side in some kind of argument.

"Well," Sylvia said to Brady, smiling at Winston, "you know, some people pay extra for that."

Winston grinned back, and Sylvia found herself thinking

that, as a younger man, Santa Claus must have been quite hand-some.

"Those are pretty," Winston said, raising his hand to point at one of the diamond-and-sapphire earrings Sylvia was wearing. He got so close, and made the gesture so naturally, that Sylvia felt her heart pound at the possibility that he was about to brush her face. But he stopped just shy of that, at a perfectly respectable distance.

"They were my mother's," she said, smiling.

"She must have known how nice you'd look in them when she gave them to you," Winston said.

At this, Sylvia's glance flickered. Her mother hadn't actually given her the earrings. They'd come to Sylvia when she died. And even though it had been years, the thought of her mother, and her loss, still hit Sylvia, as it always did.

"Or did you swipe them from her?" Winston asked, with a grin that saw he'd caught her expression—but woefully misun-derstood it.

Brady, who knew Sylvia's story because they'd known each other since they were kids, looked at Winston like the cat who had swallowed a canary.

Before he could think of another dig at Winston, Sylvia broke in. "Actually," she said, "she passed away."

"Oh," Winston said. "Oh, I'm so sorry."

Over the years that had passed since Sylvia's mother died, when Sylvia was only sixteen, she'd had to tell this news to vari-ous people, various ways, a hundred different times. She knew what it was like when they were embarrassed to have stumbled on her loss, and she knew what it was like when they didn't want to talk about it at all. All of them said some variation of what Winston had just said—"I'm sorry." But Winston was one of the few people she'd ever heard who honestly sounded like he was sorry—not just trying to cover up his own embarrassment or move the conversation past an awkward patch.

"Thanks," Sylvia said softly.

"So," Brady said, his voice just a little bit too loud for the conversation, as if he were trying to talk over some kind of city noise, even though they were in the country, where the surroundings weren't filled with sirens and voices and the rumblings of trains anymore. "What do you do?"

Sylvia actually winced.

"What?" Brady demanded. "You're not curious?"

"Winston owns a tree business," Sylvia said.

"Oh my God," Brady said, looking at Winston as if it was him who had spoken instead of Sylvia. "Are we dealing with an actual lumberjack?"

It wasn't so much what he said, as the way he said it. Brady was an expert at this. You could never get too mad at him for what he actually said—after all, what was so bad about being a lumberjack? But he made it sound like a lumberjack was an interesting animal at the zoo, and one that couldn't really understand anything that was being said to him.

And Winston picked up on it immediately.

"You know what?" he said to Sylvia. "There's someone I've got to go say hello to."

Sylvia nodded, and Winston walked away without another glance at Brady.

"Can you believe that?" Brady said to Sylvia, watching Winston as he faded into the crowd. "What about that guy, huh?"

Sylvia glanced away from Brady and sighed. She was wondering the same thing. But probably not for the same reasons as Brady.

Fifteen

"MOMMY?" JESSIE ASKED DESTINY, looking up at her from her seat beside her at the long farm table.

Rather than protecting the other guests from the kids, by sandwiching them between her and Carl, she and Carl had adopted the strategy of protecting the kids from each other, by placing them on either side—Jessie with Destiny, and Cody with Carl. So far, it had proved to be a strong option, with both kids chatting and eating happily through the meal.

But their plan had had the effect of inflicting their kids on guests who might not otherwise have had the opportunity—or the burden—of having so much interaction with them.

And since Destiny and Carl had been seated in what was pretty clearly the "family" section of the table, that meant that they were seated directly across from Beth's mom, Nadine, and Mitzi, as well as the Allertons, Gloria and Ken.

And beside Jessie, one seat down the table from Destiny, was Gloria's apparently notorious brother, Uncle Charlie.

Except that, as far as Destiny could tell, he didn't seem to be doing much that would deserve the moniker "notorious." He was an older gentleman with a handsome, kindly face, and a shock of white hair that made Destiny wonder if his sister Gloria's blond locks were the result of a bottle, or if Uncle Charlie's premature white was the result of his secret shenanigans. So far, the most remarkable thing he'd done all evening was give Jessie the candied pansy that had come with their desserts, beautiful individual chocolate ganache tortes, decorated with raspberries and the sugared blossoms.

Which was why, it turned out, Jessie was pestering Destiny now.

"Are you going to eat that?" Jessie asked, with a glance at Destiny's sugared pansy that she clearly hoped seemed nonchalant, but did nothing to disguise the profound greed for more sweets that was never really all that hidden in her sugar-loving daughter.

"What if we split it?" Destiny asked.

Jessie craned her neck down the table. "Did Cody eat his?" she asked. "I bet he didn't even like it."

This was probably accurate, Destiny knew, but she wasn't about to authorize a request, which could lead to a seemingly endless series of meltdowns, from either Jessie or Cody.

But before she had to answer, Uncle Charlie winked at her over Jessie's head, and nodded at his own sugared pansy, which he'd pushed to the side of his plate, in a clear indication that Jessie was welcome to it.

"Jessie," Destiny said. "It looks like there's someone else who doesn't want his flower."

On high alert, Jessie glanced around the table, then broke into a beaming smile when Uncle Charlie tilted his plate toward her. With a single grab and gulp, the flower disappeared into her gullet.

"What do you say?" Destiny prompted her.

"Thank you!" Jessie chirped, as Destiny smiled her own thanks to Uncle Charlie.

But she hadn't forgotten her duties as guardian of the family harmony, as assigned by Jen. So when she realized that most of the conversation at the table for the last several minutes had been between her six-year-old and Uncle Charlie, she flashed a bright smile at Gloria Allerton.

"So, Gloria," she said, "how are you liking Blue Hill?"

Gloria made what seemed like an attempt to smile, but it was so clear that she was struggling to come up with something nice to say that Destiny quickly pivoted to another question. "Have you ever been to Michigan before?" she asked.

Gloria started to shake her head when Charlie broke in with a grin. "Well, sure," he said. "Do you remember that time Dad decided he was going to drive us all across the country one summer?"

"That was hardly a trip to Michigan," Gloria said. She opened her mouth again to go on, obviously trying to get to another subject, but Charlie wasn't having it.

"But Michigan is where the car broke down!" he said. "And you're the one who talked that lady into making us all sandwiches while Dad was trying to fix it."

Gloria looked as if she wanted to sink through the floor of the barn with embarrassment, but beside her, her husband lit up, grinning at his brother-in-law.

"That's Glory," he said. "She can talk anyone into anything. You remember when we were first dating?" he asked Gloria. "We got to the museum right before it closed, and you talked that guard into letting us go with him while he made the rounds of the rooms, to make sure everyone was gone. It was our own private tour of the museum, with no one else there. And it lasted for an hour."

At this, Gloria's face broke into the first real smile Destiny had seen from her since they met. She was surprised by its openness and warmth. And by how different it was from what seemed to be Gloria's customary expression of pride and wariness.

"Mommy," Jessie said. "When are we going home?"

"You know," Uncle Charlie answered, "I see a few more of these flowers going to waste here."

He looked meaningfully at the other side of the table, where, of all the family, only Mitzi had cleaned her dessert plate.

Jessie, who had been observing the same thing in a kind of agony over the waste of such precious treats, gave him a grateful look.

"Gloria," Uncle Charlie called. "Are you finished with that plate?"

He said it in a friendly enough voice, but the look Gloria gave him was full of suspicion, and even, Destiny thought, a trace of fear.

Uncle Charlie, however, continued on placidly, reaching for the flower on her plate. When Gloria didn't object, he dropped it neatly on Jessie's own dish.

Then he glanced at Destiny, as if he'd only just realized he should have asked permission of the parent in charge, too. *Okay?* he mouthed over Jessie's head.

Destiny smiled and nodded.

"It's going to be such a beautiful wedding," Nadine was saying. "But all weddings are beautiful, I think."

On the other side of the table, she and Gloria were sandwiched together, between Mitzi and Ken, an arrangement that Gloria, for her part, looked much less than pleased with.

"Not because of decorations and the flowers," Nadine went on, "but because they're the start of a marriage. That's what's beautiful. The promises that are made. The life that's about to begin."

There was something in Nadine's tone that seemed a little off to Destiny. The words she was saying should have been simple observations, and happy ones, given the occasion. But there was a tension in her voice, almost as if she was trying to win some kind of argument that nobody else at the table even knew she was having.

But what seemed to concern Jessie, and Uncle Charlie, the most, was the uneaten candied pansy lying on Nadine's plate.

"Do you want to ask her?" Uncle Charlie stage-whispered to Jessie, when it had become clear to both of them what their next target was. "Or should I?"

To Destiny's satisfaction, Jessie wasn't shy.

"Mrs. Dean?" she piped up. "May I have your pansy?"

"Of course, dear," Nadine said. Then she glanced down the table, noticing the pansy still left on the side of Ken's plate. "Ken," she said. "This young lady would like our pansies."

Jessie's eyes goggled at her good fortune as Ken dutifully handed his pansy over. And Uncle Charlie's also glowed with interest and admiration as Nadine passed both candy flowers over to Jessie.

When Jessie began to munch the last two flowers, more carefully this time, since she seemed to realize these were the last she would get, Uncle Charlie's attention was suddenly focused on Nadine.

"There's just nothing like it," Nadine was saying. "That bond of real love. And everything that can happen when two people decide to build their lives together, with total trust. There aren't any flowers or dresses or rings in the world that could be more beautiful than that."

Uncle Charlie, Destiny noticed, smiled at this. But Gloria, who had been listening to Nadine with evident and increasing displeasure, gave an impatient sigh.

"I'm sorry, Nadine," she said. "Even you can't really think that every single marriage in this world is a font of sweetness and light."

Destiny winced, worried about how Nadine would take this sharp comment.

But Nadine didn't seem to take it as hard as Gloria may even have meant her to. "Of course not," she said simply. "I've never heard of anyone who thinks that. And that wasn't what I meant to say. I only meant to say that when a marriage is good, there's not much that's better. At least that's been my experience."

"Well, you can only speak for yourself," Gloria said dismissively, as Ken stared down at his empty plate beside her. "Not for the rest of us."

"That's all any of us can do," Nadine agreed. "But in my experience, the foundation of a good marriage is trust. And if you don't have that, I'm not sure what you have."

"You talk about trust as if it's some magic potion," Gloria snapped. "But you can trust the wrong thing. Or the wrong person. You can build a whole life with them, and then discover that they didn't deserve to be trusted."

The tone of the conversation had gotten so fraught now that even Carl and Cody were staring across the table, eyes wide open but trying to keep still, so they wouldn't be noticed and drawn into the fray.

"But you can also ruin things with the right person," Nadine said quietly. "If you refuse to trust them."

Gloria lifted her chin and set her jaw, staring past Destiny at something in the rafters of the loft, as if she thought that, if she just concentrated hard enough, she could imagine everyone else away—or imagine herself someplace completely different.

Nadine took a deep breath and sighed.

Beside Destiny, Uncle Charlie shifted in his chair.

"Personally," he said, "I'd rather take a chance on trusting the wrong person than never take the chance to trust at all. I've been in places where no one trusts anyone. Not much good ever happens there."

As he said it, Destiny suddenly got a glimpse of the uncle Charlie that Jen might have been warned about—not because he'd suddenly turned into some kind of wild man, but because the kindly face beside her suddenly took on a thousand-yard stare, as if he was seeing things that none of the rest of them could—or would ever want to.

Nadine nodded, a smile beginning to light her face. As it did, Destiny thought how pretty she still was—and how good it was to see her smile, which had been rare in the years since her husband had died.

"Nobody asked what you think, Charles," Gloria snapped. "And you're hardly the world expert on a happy marriage."

Uncle Charlie shrugged. "That's true," he said. "But you can learn a lot about something by knowing what it's like not to have it."

In response to this, Nadine's eyes widened in recognition, then locked with Uncle Charlie's. "Sometimes," she said, "people who don't have something see it even clearer than the ones who do."

Destiny knew she was talking about what it was like to look at marriage as a widow herself. But something in Uncle Charlie's eyes, which were still locked with hers, seemed to say that he knew something about living without love, as well.

But Gloria, it seemed, had no time for any of this. She retrieved her napkin from her lap, threw it on the table in disgust, pushed her chair back, and stalked off.

Jessie, who had apparently remained unfazed by the uneasy

tenor of the conversation, gazed with laser focus at the pansy Gloria had abandoned on her plate.

Uncle Charlie looked from Jessie to the pansy, then scooped it up from his sister's plate and handed it to her.

A moment later, it had vanished into Jessie's smiling mouth.

Sixteen

"THANK YOU," BETH SAID, and gave Jen a hug.

By now, most of the guests had trickled down the stairs of the loft, out to their cars or to the two big farmhouses, if they were part of the family or wedding party. Beth had stayed close with Tom for the rest of the party, even though at some moments she felt anything but close to him—because she knew that if she parted from him for even a moment, Gloria was likely to descend on her with the prenup again.

But now even Gloria had left the Deans' small barn, and there was nobody left but the caterers, who were shifting glasses and plates into big plastic racks, to be trucked away and washed. Beth's plan was to wait long enough that even Gloria would have retreated to her room, and Beth could slip into her own without having to deal with another confrontation.

Which might, she knew, mean she had to wait a while.

Jen, who had been gathering the long ropes of flowers from the tables into cardboard boxes filled with tissue, turned and smiled. "It doesn't make any sense to wrap these up," she said. "We've got more than enough for tomorrow. But I can't stand to throw them away."

"Don't worry about anything extra," Beth said. "You've already done so much. It's so much more beautiful than I could have imagined."

Jen grinned wryly. "You should hear my dad," she said. "He's willing to admit now that I can decorate a hall. Now he wants to know, if I'm so good at decorating, why I'd start with a *barn*."

Beth grinned. "I guess it must look a little different if you've actually mucked the place out yourself."

"Maybe that's it," Jen said, settling a cardboard top on one of the large square boxes, now full of blossoms.

"Seriously," Beth said. "What are you going to do with that?"

"I don't know," Jen said, shrugging. "Maybe I'll decorate your kitchen."

"Mitzi would love that," Beth said. "She keeps telling everyone she never had anything but lemonade and gingersnaps at her wedding. Which may actually be her angling to wake up tomorrow in a boudoir of hothouse flowers."

"I wouldn't put it past her," Jen said, smiling.

Beth looked around at the familiar lines of her family's old barn, with the lovely globe and string lights Jen had had installed still hanging in the rafters, letting down a gentle, even light that made the bones of the old structure look more beautiful than they ever had to her before.

"I can't believe everything you've done here," she said. "It's better than I could even imagine."

"Thanks," Jen said, then came around the long table she had been working at to give Beth a hug. For a long moment, the two of them just held on, the way they had when they were little girls, and even being separated overnight had seemed like too long to survive, requiring all kinds of hugging and celebration when one of them padded through the hedge to find the other the next morning.

"You know what I can't believe?" Jen said, when they finally broke apart. "I can't believe this is happening at all."

"Don't tell me!" Beth said, holding up her hands. "The wedding planner's main job is not to let the bride know whatever's going wrong in the background." But as she looked at Jen's face, she realized that as the bride, she was the one currently keeping secret about what was going on in the background at this wedding.

"That's not what I mean," Jen said with a smile. "I mean, this whole thing. You in New York. Finding Tom. Coming back for this wedding. Me getting to dress the whole place up with flowers flown in from Belize."

"Oh," Beth said. She'd been so lost in the weeds of what she was going to do about Gloria that the wonder Jen was describing, of the whole long arc of her story—with Tom, but even beyond that, in her whole life, was lost on her.

But now, with Jen's words, for the first time that night, Gloria seemed to fade into the distance, as she thought about the whole scope of her life, from the dreams she and Jen and Destiny had had as girls, to the things they'd accomplished already, with Destiny's family, and Jen's new business, and her own move to the city and the memories of Tom that flooded in as she thought of it: the fancy dates he'd first planned, trying to impress her, and how relieved they'd been when they both realized they'd just rather order Turkish food from the restaurant below her building and hang out at home together, the way his eyes had widened with admiration when he first saw her come out of her room wearing a formal dress to attend a gala with him—and the way his eyes still lit up every time he saw her, no matter how dressed up she was or wasn't. And that same look in his eyes when, almost a year to the day after they'd started dating, she opened up the bag of Turkish food he'd just ordered to find a ring inside.

Suddenly, she felt a wave of gratitude—not just for the good things that had come to her in life, but for the friends, like Jen, who had stuck with her whether things looked good or bad, and for the love between her and Tom, which was what they were all there to celebrate.

"I mean," Jen said, her smile broadening, "this is a far cry from those days when we used to grow a zinnia patch out behind the barn."

"And sell them by the side of the road for five cents a stem!" Beth said.

"We should start an import business," Jen said. "Market them in Brooklyn, as free-range zinnias."

"That actually might work," Beth said. "And I bet we could get more than five cents a stem."

"Always thinking," Jen said, tapping her head. She slid her arm around Beth's waist. "But let's get you married off first. What are you still doing out here?"

For an instant, Beth considered letting it all out: everything Gloria and Tom had said to her, and the jumble of thoughts that had been in her head ever since. But now she didn't want to drag those thoughts into the same space in her head as her sweet memories of Tom. She just shook her head.

"Let's get you to bed," Jen said. "That's *actually* my number one job as wedding planner."

Arm in arm, they took the short, cold walk to Beth's kitchen stairs. As the glow of the kitchen became clear on their approach, Beth saw with relief that there was nobody there. The coast was clear for her to slip up to her room without a run-in with Gloria.

"You want to come in?" Beth asked.

Jen shook her head. "I'm just going over to our place," she

said. "Going to make sure everything's all set for tomorrow morning."

"Thanks again," Beth said. "I'll never be able to thank you for everything you're doing. But what means the most"—she paused, surprised by the emotion that welled up in her throat—"is that you're here," she finished.

"I can't wait to see you get married," Jen said, giving her another quick hug, but bouncing on her feet from the cold. "It's going to be beautiful."

"Because of you," Beth said with a smile, then darted up the kitchen stairs.

The house was absolutely silent, except for the noises of the house that had become so familiar with time that they hardly seemed like noise anymore: the breathing of the furnace through the vents, the faint creaks of the house as it adjusted to the falling temperatures.

Quickly, before anyone could see her, Beth went through the kitchen and up the stairs. The hallway to her room was dark and deserted, with no light spilling from under the door of any room but her own.

With a sense of relief, she took a deep breath and began to pad down the long rug that ran the length of the hall.

But when she laid her hand on the knob to open the door to her own room, and a ray of light began to spread throughout the hall, she heard a voice behind her, almost as if someone had managed to follow her silently, all the way up the stairs.

"Beth!" Gloria whispered. Was it Beth's imagination, or did her voice really sound something like a hiss? "I've been waiting to talk with you."

Before Beth could even work out where in the world Gloria

had been standing—lurking in the dark hallway? In the dark behind the door to Gloria's own room?—Gloria had shoved her way into Beth's room and taken up a place between Beth and her own bed.

Not wanting to wake up her mother or Mitzi, Beth closed the door, then turned back to face Gloria.

Of course, she had the prenup out again, waving it like some kind of a flag between them. "You've had your time to think this over," Gloria said. "Now it's time to sign."

Before, Gloria had at least been trying to convince Beth. But now she was using a tone that made it clear that, when they got down to it, Beth was nothing but a servant who couldn't do anything but take her orders.

And that started some kind of slow burning fire in Beth's belly.

She took the prenup from Gloria, watching the flicker of triumph in Gloria's eyes when she did.

But then she dropped it to the floor.

"I won't be signing this, Gloria," she said. "Not today, and not ever."

Gloria's smirk of triumph turned quickly to an O of surprise. She crouched down to retrieve the legal document, and as she did, Beth swung the door to her room open.

"Just because you have a terrible marriage," she said, "doesn't mean that Tom and I will." As she said it, she couldn't quite believe the words were coming out of her mouth. But that didn't stop them from coming.

"Now, if you'll excuse me," she said, "I need to get some sleep. I'm getting married in the morning."

Gloria's face was a mask of fury. For a moment, Beth worried that she might refuse to leave, and Beth would have to decide whether she was going to physically drag her mother-in-law-to-be out of her room, or flee her own room, herself.

But then Gloria lifted her chin and stalked out.

As soon as she did, tears began to leak down Beth's face.

She sank onto her bed.

Oh God, she prayed. *This isn't how I ever thought my wedding would be. What should I do? Please help me.*

Seventeen

"JEN," JARED SAID BREATHLESSLY, jogging through the snow to catch up with her. "Wait up."

Jen looked around. The snow was still falling so heavily that it was getting pretty impossible to see clearly for more than a few feet in any direction, but she still could have sworn that nobody was out in the yard when she'd finally emerged from the Dean family's small barn, after the final caterer had taken their final chafing dish out into the night and their headlights had begun to light up the snow, turning it shining and weird as they backed their cars up and headed slowly down the driveway in the increasingly treacherous snowfall.

How had Jared gotten there? Where had he been lurking?

And why, after all these years, did she still have the urge to greet him with a kiss?

Annoyed with herself, she shook her head, tromping on through the snow as if he hadn't said anything.

That didn't stop him from catching up with her. And when he did, even in the darkness, and with the thick flakes swirling around them, she could see the way his hands reached for her, almost instinctively—and the way he checked himself, jamming them deep into the pockets of his unbuttoned parka as he struggled to keep up with her through the drifts, which were now barking their shins.

At least she wasn't the only one who was having trouble re-membering they weren't together anymore, Jen told herself. And then she wondered—was that really a good thing?

Think about Ed, she told herself, and tried to bring up one of her favorite moments with him: the time he'd shown up at her house with a bag full of fried chicken when she'd had a tough day at work, or the first time he'd kissed her, after they'd been hanging out with friends at the local bar.

But when she tried to bring those memories up, her mind just seemed to fill up with snow like the flakes that were still fall-ing all around them.

"Where are you going?" Jared asked. "Shouldn't you get some sleep?"

Jen bit back the retort that she'd been remembering to get enough sleep very well for the past several *years*, thank you very much, without him around to remind her. Instead, she just said, "I've got to move the horses."

"The horses?" Jared said, his voice rising in surprise, which broke quickly into a laugh. "They part of the ceremony?"

"I hope not," Jen said. "That's the point. I've got to get them out of Dad's barn over to the Deans'. Dad was going to do it in the morning, but I want to get it done tonight."

"You want a hand?" Jared asked.

Jen didn't stop her steady progress through the snow, but she took a mental pause, debating. Of course she wanted a hand. It would be a lot easier getting two horses out of their stalls and situated in their new quarters with two people than one. But did she really want to have to deal with Jared any more tonight?

Before she came up with an answer, they arrived at the door of her father's barn.

"I don't know," she said. "I think it might be bad luck for you to see the place all done up before tomorrow."

In the light that poured down through the snow from the flood on the peak of the barn, Jared grinned. "Well," he said cheerfully, "we're not the ones getting married."

Jen was surprised how hard this hit her. If you'd asked her a minute before, she would have snapped back that *of course* she knew that she and Jared weren't the ones getting married. That fact had been driven home to her daily for years. It wasn't something she was likely to forget.

But when she heard him say it out loud, her stomach gave a sick lurch, which knocked her off-balance so completely that all she could think to do was turn away from him, grab the door of the barn, and swing it open—to get away from him, if nothing else.

For the first moment after the door swung open, the two of them gasped together in unison. Jared had seen the place earlier that afternoon, and Jen had seen it in her head a thousand times before that. But something about the great barn, filled with flowers and white fabric, with all the white chairs lined up in their even rows, and the arbor of flowers at their apex, in the half-light of full evening, with the glimmers of endless flakes falling past outside every window, left Jen breathless.

And then, as her gaze dropped from the peak of the barn, where the globe lights suspended from the rafters cast the light that let them see, down to the details of the setup, she gasped again.

Because instead of waiting patiently for her in their stalls, where Jen had left them each a celebratory extra cup of wedding oats, her family's two horses, Henrietta and Napoleon, were both standing in the main aisle of her setup, munching happily on the flowers that bedecked the chairs at the end of each row. They had almost reached the door. And with a single glance, Jen took in the fact that they had stripped each chair clean of the lovely blossoms that Pamela and Lindy had installed that afternoon— not just from the chairs, but from the arbor that formed the centerpiece of the entire ceremony. In fact, since that was closest to the stalls that Napoleon and Henrietta had escaped from, the arbor had almost certainly been their first course.

"Henrietta!" Jen hissed. "Napoleon!"

Henrietta, a handsome sorrel mare with a beautiful reddish coat, looked up at Jen with her large, kind brown eyes. But the alarm in Jen's voice didn't stop Henrietta's steady munch on a gorgeous white dahlia for a single beat.

And Napoleon, a blue roan stallion with a brunet mane and a silver sheen to his brown flanks, who in general had a reasonably winning disposition, swallowed a sprig of snapdragons as if nobody had even said anything.

Jen's stomach seemed to drop past her body, well below her feet, down into some secret ring of hell reserved only for wedding planners. But that was only to make room for the rising panic that almost immediately filled her chest, then her head, then seemed to engulf the room around her and continue rising, until she felt like she was standing at the bottom of an ocean of it.

She couldn't even decide how to count up the scope of the disaster. What was worse: All the hours that Pamela Lindy had spent choosing and tying and trimming and arranging the flowers that were now being digested in the gullets of the greedy beasts? All the money Beth and Tom had shelled out to fly those flowers in from points all around the world, just so they could be there for their special day tomorrow? The way her father would guffaw when he found out? The looks of mild contempt on the faces of the New Yorkers when they filed in, fake smiles pasted on their faces, eyebrows slightly raised, as if to say they hadn't expected anything much more than a few fronds of cheap baby's breath for decorations at a backwoods wedding like this, anyway? The look on Beth's face when Jen had to tell her that the flowers they'd been planning for and dreaming about for so long . . . were gone?

Jared, who had come in behind her, didn't even seem to have noticed the two giant beasts happily chomping on the decorations for tomorrow's wedding. Instead, he'd stopped just inside the door and was currently gazing up at the lights swinging gently from the rafters above, a dreamy look on his face.

"Jared!" Jen said. "Can you help me with this?"

She hadn't been planning to tramp down the silk runner that had already been laid out from the door to the arbor at the end of the aisle. Her plan had been to skirt the whole setup, heading for the horses' stalls, and not leave any trace of her clodhopper work boots for tomorrow. For a moment, she had a crazy idea that she should take her boots off before she stepped onto the runner now, but there was no way she was going to go toe to toe with a several-ton beast, no matter how docile, without a pair of shoes to protect her own feet. And as she looked down the way, she could see clear evidence of hoofprints on the delicate fabric already.

"Napoleon," she barked, then whistled his command to come to her.

The old stallion's ears twitched, but he didn't make a move—other than to fill his soft lips with a healthy portion of soft green leaves, since the arrangement he was standing in front of was now completely denuded of any blooms, and Jen's imprecations had apparently made him uneasy about moving on to the next one.

An instant later, all her niceties thrown to the wind, Jen had tromped down the aisle and grabbed him by the halter.

With her now there in person, instead of shouting from the end of the aisle, Napoleon was all cooperation. He even looked at her with something approaching gratitude, as if he was wondering if she was the one he had to thank for that evening's enormous good fortune.

"Jen," Jared called, running down the aisle, where he quickly caught Henrietta the same way Jen had captured Napoleon. "What's going on?"

Jen locked eyes with him, her own eyes wide with shock. "They ate all the flowers," she said. "All of them. All the way down the aisle."

She wasn't sure what she expected from him, whether she wanted him to gather her in a comforting hug, or look as shocked as she did, or begin to heap curses on the heads of the two errant horses.

But instead of doing any of that, Jared just threw back his head and began to laugh and laugh.

Eighteen

"MOMMY?" JESSIE ASKED. HER eyes were so heavy with sleep that she could barely keep them open, but somehow she still managed to have a wide-eyed expression of wonder every time they did flicker back to life.

"Yes, honey?" Destiny asked.

She was sitting on the edge of Jessie's bed, trying to keep the stiff fabric of the formal dress from rustling too much and scaring the sandman away. Both the kids had fallen asleep on the long drive home from the Deans', partly because of the late hour, but perhaps because the snow had been so thick around the car windows that there was absolutely nothing out there for them to see.

She half expected Jessie to drift off midthought, as she often did. But as Jessie had been getting older, the strength of her trains of thought had gotten stronger and stronger, so that Destiny had to be careful not to get involved in bedtime discussions that opened so many possibilities, good or bad, that Jessie no longer wanted to sleep—which was never her favorite activity to begin with.

And even though Jessie's eyelids still drooped, this thought was strong enough to struggle to the surface, even against the powerful impulse to sleep, after all the excitement of the night.

"What is New York City?" Jessie asked.

Just in case Jessie's eyes popped open again, Destiny suppressed her smile. Obviously, Jessie had been hearing some of the chatter from the other guests that night.

And although Destiny knew better, she couldn't resist asking a question herself, as she sometimes did, to get her kids to think for themselves, instead of always asking someone else for the answers. Not to mention the fact that, at ages three and six, their answers were frequently hilarious. "What do you think it is, sweetie?" she asked.

Jessie's eyes stayed closed, but they squinched slightly in thought. "Is it like Cedar Point?" she said, naming a famous Midwestern amusement park.

"Kind of," Destiny said, unable to hide her smile now, and pretty sure that Jessie was going down for the count.

"Or," Jessie said, rallying for a minute, "is it like heaven, where some people live but we can't go there yet?"

Some of what her kids said to Destiny made her smile. Some of it, like this, stopped her in her tracks. Instead of answering, she leaned down to give Jessie a kiss.

"You know what?" she said. "I bet we can find New York in your encyclopedia. Do you want to look it up in the morning?"

But by now, Jessie had wandered off into slumber, her hand open on the pillow beside her face.

Jessie's questions jumbled in her head, Destiny wandered out of her room, and caught a glimpse of herself in the full-length mirror that was propped up at the end of the hall, because, for years, neither she nor Carl had ever managed to get around to fastening it properly to the wall.

She barely recognized the woman in the reflection. Even without her high-heeled shoes, which she'd kicked off in trade for boots before they'd even left the Dean barn, the shape of her dress hugged her curves, making her look like some smoky character in an old black-and-white noir thriller. The dim light of the hallway erased all traces of the peanut butter she'd been worrying about all night. And her hair, still miraculously working for once, curled around her face in all the right places.

Destiny couldn't tell if the woman she saw reflected in the glass was a glimpse of who she really was: the smart, sophisticated, even beautiful woman who was usually hidden under sweatpants and fanny packs and, let's face it, more peanut butter. Or if the fancy strange she saw in the mirror was the impostor, and the frazzled mom in a mismatched outfit she was used to looking back at was the real thing.

As she shook her head and sighed, looking away, Carl tiptoed out of Cody's room, where he'd just been putting Cody down.

"Hey, gorgeous," he said, greeting her with a warm kiss.

Destiny tried to kiss him back, but she didn't feel like herself, caught between the woman in the glass and her daytime reflection.

"You tired?" Carl asked.

Destiny didn't know if she was tired or not. But that was an easier explanation to give him than the explanation she couldn't even seem to be able to find to give herself.

"You want a cup of tea?" he asked.

She didn't particularly, but the cup of tea was a sweet ritual that Carl had developed, a little thing he liked to do for her after the kids were in bed, and she never liked to refuse it. "Sure," she said, and followed him down the hall to the kitchen, where she perched on one of the banged-up stools that surrounded their kitchen counter while he began to rummage around for the water and pans and tea bags.

When he finally set the cup of tea in front of her, she realized that she must have been staring out the back window, into the thick white flakes of snow, her mind wandering over everything she had and everything she might have had, all that time.

And she realized that Carl had noticed.

"You're not just tired, are you?" he said, looking at her closely but somewhat warily.

Destiny shook her head.

"What's wrong?" he asked.

She could tell from the tightness in his voice that he thought she was angry at him—maybe, Destiny realized, because she had snapped at him before they even got to the party, although that was now the furthest thing in the world from her mind.

"Oh," she said. "It's not you."

She could see the tension go out of Carl's frame at these words, and the sight of it just made her feel worse. Everything she'd wanted—she decided that this man, and these kids, and this house, were worth more than all of it. And was this what it all added up to? Not some great romance, or even a family in harmony, but him bracing himself for her to launch into another salvo about whatever her frustrations with him were in that very moment?

She sighed and watched his shoulders square again. Well, maybe trying to explain it to him would help her explain it to herself—or at least get her thoughts out in the open, where they often didn't seem quite so important and serious. "It's about me," she said. "My whole life."

From the look on his face, she could see that this had somehow been an even worse answer than he had been bracing himself for.

"What do you mean?" he said, obviously trying not to snap at her—and not exactly succeeding. "As far as I know, I'm a pretty big part of your whole life."

And maybe that was the problem flashed across Destiny's mind, as annoyance rose in her in response to his tone.

"You know I always wanted to go to New York," Destiny said. "Try a totally different kind of life. See if I could make it on my own."

When they'd been kids, Carl had even dreamed about this with her. He had his own plans, she remembered. "You had ideas like that, too," she said. "You were going to go to Nashville and see if anybody would let you lay down guitar on one of those country tracks."

Carl shook his head impatiently. "Sure," he said. "But that was kid stuff."

"Not for me," Destiny shot back.

"Oh, come on," Carl said impatiently. "What has New York got that's so special? As far as I can tell, the people from there look a lot like you and me."

"I don't know," Destiny said, her voice almost breaking in frustration.

When he heard the sorrow in her voice, Carl's own expression softened. And, somehow, that was enough for a memory to come to the surface of Destiny's mind: a young woman in a black sheath, munching on a pastry in front of a window full of diamonds.

"Do you remember that movie *Breakfast at Tiffany's*?" Destiny asked.

A smile, laced with mild exasperation, crossed Carl's lips. "You made me watch it," he said. "Back when we were dating."

"I always thought," Destiny said, discovering the words for herself as she said them, "that maybe one day, I'd get to go do that, too. Buy myself a croissant from some little bakery, and finish it while I'm staring in that window."

Until she finished, Carl had been looking at her with real attention, as if she might finally be giving him something he could work with. When she fell silent, he looked at her for a moment longer, as if waiting for her to get to the point.

When he realized there wasn't one, his expression of mild exasperation started to veer toward serious anger.

"That's it?" he said. "That's what you want, instead of"—he paused for a moment, recalling her own words to shoot them back at her—"your whole life?"

"I didn't say that," Destiny said. "I—"

"Well, I guess I don't know what you're saying, then," Carl said. "You know what's not in New York City? Me," he said, his voice rising.

"Carl," Destiny said, glancing back toward the bedrooms. "The kids."

"And the kids," Carl added. "You're not really trying to tell me you'd rather go look in a window full of some jewelry you'd never wear, all by yourself, than be here with the kids and me and everything we've built together?"

Destiny set her jaw. Then she opened her mouth to object. But she didn't do it fast enough.

"You would," Carl said, his voice suddenly full of a weird kind of wonder. "Some part of you actually would."

"Not forever," Destiny said. "It's just that, sometimes—"

"You know what?" Carl said, tossing the towel he'd used to hold the hot pan back onto the stovetop. "I think it's better if we end this conversation here."

"Carl—" Destiny said as he began to stalk away.

"And you know what else?" he said, turning back. "You make it sound like me and the kids are holding you prisoner here, or something. But we're not." He spread his arms out. "If you really want to get out of here that bad," he said, "you could still go."

The way he said it, and the way he walked off, made Destiny feel like it was some kind of threat. Or maybe like he even wished she would, if this was how she really felt.

But she didn't know how she really felt.

Of course she wouldn't trade her family in for a life in the city.

But what about all those dreams she'd had when they were young? Maybe it wasn't about any one jewelry store but those dreams she'd had for some other kind of life, or even just a glimpse of one, something of her own, however small, where she wasn't someone's wife, or mom, but just herself.

Was that really kid stuff?

Had it really meant nothing at all?

Nineteen

"YOU SURE IT'S LOCKED?" Jared asked with a grin, giving the stall he'd just led Napoleon into a good shake to make sure it was securely fastened—unlike the faulty door at her dad's barn that had let both the family steeds out to feast on Beth's wedding flowers.

In the stall, Napoleon whickered and tossed his head, as if he couldn't believe she hadn't given him another noseful of oats as dessert, after all the hundreds of blooms he and Henrietta had already disposed of down their gullets.

"Not funny yet," Jen said, patting Henrietta on the nose as the old mare shifted nervously in the unfamiliar stall.

Then Jen heaved a deep sigh and turned away. When she'd discovered the carnage in the wedding hall, she'd at least had the comfort of an immediate problem to solve: how to get the two horses out of there, and over to their temporary quarters.

But now that she'd done that, the question of what to do next rushed in at her. And all she could see was an empty barn. Searching for answers, her mind wandered out of it, past the walls, into the night. The boxes of flowers from the rehearsal dinner that she'd carried out the doors earlier that evening popped into her mind, but there weren't many of them, and the flowers in the vine-like ropes of greenery that had lain down the length of each table were only tossed into the greens sporadically. There were hardly enough to rebuild the centerpieces of the arrangements—or in some cases, replace them completely, since in the first arrangements the horses had encountered, they'd gobbled up almost everything, including the greens. And even when they'd become more discriminating as they wandered down the line, evidencing a strong preference for the soft blossoms over the less tender greens, many of the remaining greens had still suffered a fatal crushing, even if they hadn't been actually consumed.

Her mind wheeled out into the night, mentally ransacking the house, the yard, which would be full of flowers if it were only six, or even four months from now. Her thoughts drifted down the snow-filled road toward town, which boasted no local florist she could make an emergency call to. And with the storm still in full force, getting any farther in the morning, to one of the bigger towns even farther away was out of the question.

As she fought the panic that still rose in her chest, tempting her to give all her thoughts to it and give up on any hope of solution, her mind, in desperation, started to roam in the opposite direction: not toward the cozy house, or the lights of town, but out past the barn, where the fields began, and beyond them, the strips of pine forest that still divided property from property in many of these parts.

And that's where it stopped.

"The pine stands," she said, turning to Jasper, her eyes wide.

"Huh?" Jasper asked, surprised.

"The pine stands," Jen repeated, grabbing a pair of clippers from Mrs. Dean's workbench, and heading toward the door. "I bet I can bring back enough branches to fill in what's been lost in the arrangements. And I think I saw bittersweet out that way this fall, as well." The bittersweet branches, with their orange berries in yellow petals that dried to a rich gold each autumn, would add a pop of color, if she could just find them.

"Wait up," Jared said, jogging after her as she strode out the back door of the barn, her boots beginning to make a satisfying crunch in the snow. To her relief, despite the thick flakes that would make it almost white-out conditions in a car, she could still see the field line that ran out the half acre or so to the pine woods that she and Beth had spent so many days playing in as girls, hiding behind the copper-colored trunks of the trees, or resting in the soft pine needles that piled under their branches.

She tried to push the fact that it had also been a favorite meeting spot for her and Jared out of her mind.

But apparently, she wasn't the only one who had thought of it. "Wow," Jared said, when they reached the edge of the stand, a mix of full-grown trees and yew bushes that Jen quickly calculated would yield at least two new kinds of greens for the arrangements. "It looks exactly the same."

Jen's heart twisted a bit as they stepped inside the fringe of the branches. They'd never done that before without Jared pulling her in for a kiss. And she could see by the way he looked at her that she wasn't the only one who had thought of this, either.

In response, she caught the nearest branch, ran her gloved hand down to a point where it got too thick to be decorative, then snipped it cleanly, pushed it into Jared's arms, and crouched down to examine the fronds of the leggy yew bush growing wild at the edge of the little forest.

When she did, she felt a rain of snow on her head.

When she looked up, brushing it away, another gentle spray of snow landed on her face. Through the falling flakes, she could see Jared's grin—and the branch he had been shaking over her head to douse her.

He clearly expected to get some kind of rise out of her, but Jen knew him too well to give him the satisfaction. Instead, she coolly harvested several boughs of yew with a set of steady snips, then rose and piled them in Jared's arms along with the soft pine.

"As wedding planner," she said, "it's against my policy to harm a guest."

"Oh, it is, is it?" Jared said, as if this was a very interesting invitation.

Jen nodded, but as Jared reached up to shower her with the snow from another branch, she raised her hand. "After the wedding, though," she said, "my contractual obligations are finished."

"And what's that mean?" Jared asked, his hand lowering.

Jen reached for the same branch, then flicked it so he was suddenly covered with glittering snow. "Watch your back," she said.

Jared grinned as if she'd just handed him a million bucks.

"Jen," he said. "It's been too long."

Jen could feel the old familiar pull toward him, but the stronger it got, the more something else rose in her, too: a clearer and clearer awareness of the stubborn fact that, although it felt like a day hadn't passed since she saw him last, a lot of days had. Years of them. Without any word, and without any real explanation.

And if she let herself go now, she had no promise at all that he wouldn't take off at the end of the weekend and leave her on her own for years more.

"Whose fault is that?" she said, turning away to trim another set of likely boughs.

"You know, Jen," he said. "I never wanted to leave you."

Jen piled a bunch of branches in his arms, her eyebrows raised in a way that clearly communicated the fact that she thought he had a funny way of showing that.

Jared took a deep breath. "I didn't think I could ask you to go with me," he said. "I had no idea what I was doing."

Jen tilted her head to show that at least she agreed with that analysis of the situation.

"Jen," Jared said.

Finally, she turned to look at him.

"I just want to know . . ." he said, then trailed off, as if he hadn't known what he wanted to say to begin with, or perhaps thought better of asking once the words came to his lips. "I just want to know, are you happy?"

Deep in Jen's pocket, her phone began to vibrate and ring. Startled, she began to pat her sides, hunting for its precise location.

"Sorry," she said. "Who would call this late?" Her mind began to spin with possible disasters. Had something happened to the guests in one of the houses? In town? Had someone from the wedding party, God forbid, wandered into the half-ruined wedding hall?

But when she pulled it out, she saw Ed's photograph on the screen.

"Get it," Jared said, nodding. "It must be important."

With a deep breath, Jen answered the phone.

"Hey, honey," she said. As she did, her eyes locked with Jared's.

"Hey, babe," Ed said cheerfully. "How's my rock star? You got everything all buttoned up yet? You know, you need to get your rest."

Jen closed her eyes and shook her head. "Not quite yet," she said.

She tried to keep her voice light, hoping she'd just be able to say a quick goodbye and get off the line, but she couldn't escape the strength of Ed's powers of observation, even over the phone.

"Babe," he said. "Is anything wrong?"

Jared had laughed at her predicament, but Ed's sympathy made tears well up in Jen's eyes—which was the last thing, she realized, that she wanted in this situation. "It's just—" she began, then felt exhausted with the task of trying to explain everything to Ed, who she knew would be so worried about her that she'd have to spend time comforting him by telling him she was all right, instead of just going ahead and solving the problem. "There've been a few kinks in my plans."

"Nothing serious?" Ed said, his voice just as alarmed as she'd known it would be.

"No, no," she said soothingly, trying not to glance at Jared again. "It's fine. It's all gonna be fine." She wished she felt half as confident as she sounded.

"That's what I like to hear," Ed said, pleased. "Well, I guess I shouldn't keep you too long."

"Thanks for calling, baby," Jen said.

"You know I'll always call you," Ed said.

"I do," Jen said.

"Sweet dreams," Ed said.

"You too," Jen told him, and hung up.

Shaking her head, Jen put the phone back in her pocket.

Then she locked eyes with Jared. As she did, her stomach did the familiar backflip it always had when she met his eyes, from the time she was fourteen—or maybe even earlier. By this time tonight, she'd been through too much to pretend it wasn't happening. But that didn't mean she had to do anything about it. In fact, she thought, what she needed to do was the opposite— remind herself exactly why things could never work with them, despite what her emotions did, without her permission. And he didn't have the right to ask her questions like "Are you happy?" unless she had the right to ask him some questions of her own.

"Why did you go to Texas?" she asked simply.

"You know that," Jared said, caught off guard. "I got such a good job offer. They were gonna let me run—"

"—your own part of the company," Jen finished for him. She'd heard it a million times, both from him and in her own head, after he left. At the time, she'd never argued with him about it. He'd just acted like it was the most sensible thing in the world, and so, even though her heart was aching, she'd tried to act like a grown-up, too—even though neither of them, just out of college, really had much idea of what that meant. At first, she'd thought he'd come to his senses as soon as he'd been there awhile, realize how much he missed her, and come back or ask her to come with him. And when that hadn't happened, it had been too late to ask all the questions that crowded in.

"But that's not what I mean," Jen said. "Why did you go, when I'm here?"

Jared's eyes got wide, the whites showing even in the dark. It was clear he didn't have an answer to that question—at least not one he knew how to give her.

"Are you happy?" she asked.

Even though it was the question he had just asked her, Jared looked as if he was hearing it now, about himself, for the first time. Maybe as if it was something he hadn't even allowed himself to ask in the privacy of his own mind.

His eyes got wide, and he glanced from side to side, as if he thought some other member of the wedding party might be about to jump out from behind one of the frozen pines and rescue him from the question.

"Um," he said. "I don't really know how to answer that."

Jen turned back to lop off another batch of branches, then added a few fistfuls of yew for good measure, and put them on top of the massive pile Jared was now carrying. He was a big guy, she calculated quickly, but that was probably as much as made sense for now.

She snipped down a few more giant branches, maybe even big enough to cover up some of the damage to the arbor at the front of the barn, gathered them up in her arms, and headed back toward the lights of the house, which were getting dimmer and dimmer as the snow got thicker.

As soon as Jared realized she was going, he loped along to catch up with her. "Have you been watching Tom and Beth?" he asked.

Jen raised her eyebrows again. She'd been doing little other than watching Tom and Beth for what seemed like years, although it'd been more like months.

"They seem happy," Jared said. "That looks good to me."

Jen ducked her head against the driving snow, just trying to press on against the wind.

"You didn't tell me," Jared said. "Are you happy, Jen?"

Jen just tramped on through the snow. The sound of the wind was loud enough that maybe he'd think his words had blown away on the wind.

She didn't have an answer to give him.

Because that would mean she would have to have an answer to give herself.

Twenty

SYLVIA HAD HOPED THAT at just before six a.m., her normal running time, she might be the only one in the Dean family kitchen. And when she first stepped in, it was still so shadowy in the faintest light of morning that she thought she was.

But Mitzi's voice quickly disabused her of that notion.

"Are those pajamas?" she asked. "Or your bridesmaid's dress?"

Sylvia caught the slight note of teasing in Mitzi's voice. She wasn't some hayseed who couldn't tell the difference between a formal gown and a pair of pj's. She was tweaking Sylvia about her running gear: a set of skintight hyperpolar thermal tights and a matching zippered jacket with a double-high funnel neck, all in a deep black with a few carefully chosen electric-blue stripes that made the whole ensemble reminiscent of a deep-sea-diving outfit.

Sylvia smiled at the older woman's moxie. "I'm going running," she said.

As Sylvia's eyes adjusted to the dim light in the kitchen, she could see Mitzi leaning against the counter, nursing a cup of coffee—and raising a single eyebrow. "You see it's still snowing?" she asked.

"Snowing" was a polite word for it. The storm that had been setting in when Sylvia went to bed that night didn't seem to have lost any vigor in the intervening hours. In fact, it seemed like it might have grown stronger. Thick flakes still fell in white sheets beyond the snug farmhouse windows.

But Sylvia knew her gear, ridiculous as it might look to Mitzi, was the most highly rated winter wear you could buy. The brand had pictures of climbers wearing it during ascents on Mount Kilimanjaro. She'd bought it because she always liked to have the best, but she'd always felt just a little bit sheepish wearing it around the streets of Manhattan, where the steepest ascent was to the rocky outcrops amidst the greener fields of Central Park, and the temperature rarely dropped much below freezing, even in the depth of winter. And some part of her was tickled, now, at the opportunity to wear it in conditions that, if they weren't exactly Arctic, were at least a bit more polar than Times Square.

"I never let the weather stop me in Manhattan," Sylvia said, pulling her high-tech ear warmers down to cover her ears, and slipping on her equally high-tech gloves. "Why would I let it stop me now?"

"This isn't Manhattan weather," Mitzi observed. But even though Mitzi barely held back a mildly mocking smile, Sylvia could see a bit of respect in her eyes, as if the fancy lady from New York City was proving to be a bit tougher than Mitzi might initially have realized.

"I'm just going to do a few miles, then loop back," Sylvia assured her as she dropped her sunglasses on and slipped out the door.

When she first stepped out, she felt like some kind of superhero. The blast of snow and cold stung her cheeks and lips, which were pretty much the only skin exposed to the elements. But the rest of her was perfectly toasty warm—as if she'd just developed some kind of superhuman immunity to the cold.

The jolt of it spurred her to sprint down the back porch steps—which was also the only way to get down them, because they were pretty much lost in the six or seven inches of snow that had fallen during the night.

But that just meant she had to high step when she got down into the yard and started to follow the trail of the drive down to the road—which made it an even better workout.

And the road was hardly obliterated by the snow, as much of it as there was. The ditches might be full of soft banks, but the road itself cut a clear line between the fields on either side, and although it looked like not a single car had driven down it yet, there were places where the winds of the storm had swept it almost clean. Of course, that meant there were also places where the snow had piled up two or three feet, but she was nimble enough to navigate where a car, or even a big truck, might have trouble—which only increased her sense of superpower status.

When the pedometer at her wrist showed a quarter of a mile, she still felt like she'd barely started, and she turned down a likely lane, marked with a line of tall, skinny trees on either side that the farmers had apparently decided to spare from the axe when they were carving out their fields.

It wound and split for another half a mile before she even began to feel winded. And she made it a whole two miles before she even thought about turning back.

But when she did, she suddenly felt immensely tired.

And when she looked back along the snowy road she'd been pounding down, she suddenly had no recollection of exactly how she'd gotten there.

No matter, she told herself. It couldn't be that complicated to get back, even if all she did was follow her own trail.

But as she comforted herself with that thought, she realized that the prints she'd just left were already being scoured away by the gusts of wind.

And for the first time, she felt cold.

She set off at a brisk jog, since of course her temperature would be expected to drop as soon as she stopped moving. But now she couldn't seem to shake the cold, which seemed to seep deeper into her bones the more gulps of cold air she breathed in to keep herself going—until, whether it was because of the cold or a tightening in her chest in response to her alarm, it became hard for her to get enough breath, and her shivering, which had come at first in starts and stops, was so constant she could barely think.

In the meantime, she couldn't tell if she had made any progress at all—either from the spot where she had turned back, which she couldn't see on the road behind her, or toward the spot where she'd turned off the main road, which she still couldn't see from here.

She had a brief thought that since she had her phone, now was the time to give up and call an Uber. When she realized how crazy an idea that was, this far out from any city, and in the middle of a snow squall, she laughed aloud.

Then, suddenly, she felt very alone.

As she did, what looked like a ball of snow appeared through the scrim of trees that defined the winding road. At first she looked at it in consternation, wondering if it was some kind of earthbound snow tornado, known only in the hinterlands of Michigan. But then, through the muffling thickness of her ear warmers, she made out the rumble of an engine.

A truck, she realized. It was a truck.

As soon as it came into full view around a bend in the road, she began to wave her arms, calculating that at least whoever it was could tell her how far she was from the main road, and if she'd taken a wrong turn on her way back to it.

And sure enough, as the truck rolled up on her, it slowed, and a window rolled down.

"Winston!" she gasped when she saw the familiar face within.

Winston, who had rolled the window down with an inquiring grin, suddenly looked surprised and disturbed.

"It's Sylvia," Sylvia said, her teeth chattering. Why would she expect him to recognize her, all dressed up in sunglasses and scuba gear against the snow?

But that apparently wasn't what had caused his alarm.

"Get in," he said, his voice suddenly gruff. "You're going to freeze out there."

"I just need to know how far I am from the Fitzgerald—" Sylvia started, but Winston shook his head, cutting her off.

"Your lips are blue," he informed her. "Get in the truck."

Sylvia had only stopped moving for a few moments, but the cold felt like if she waited even a second longer, she might be frozen to the spot forever.

With great effort, as if she was wading through molasses instead of freshly fallen snow, she made her way around the back, and climbed up into his cab.

"What are you wearing?" Winston asked. "A scuba suit?"

But Sylvia just looked at him, eyes wide, so cold she couldn't talk.

"Hang on," Winston said. "I'm taking you home."

Instead of turning the truck around, he gunned the engine, and a handful of curves and hills later, he seemed to veer off the road completely, into what looked like a field studded with large, bare trees. But a moment later, as they came over a low rise, a pretty white farmhouse appeared.

Winston drove up to the front porch, came around the side of the truck, and opened the door. Sylvia tried gamely to jump down, but when she stumbled in the snow, he caught her under the arm and half carried her up the steps.

Inside, he led her over to a rocking chair beside a large black stove, which was pouring off enough heat to fill the entire room. When she sank down in it, he went over to a big hand-carved wooden chest and pulled out an armful of blankets. He piled three blankets on top of her, then knelt down to pull off her boots.

"How are you doing?" he asked. "Sylvia?"

Sylvia nodded and tried to speak again. This time her voice was weak, but at least it came out. "Thanks," she said.

Winston let out a deep sigh, like he was the one who had been worried he couldn't talk.

"Damn, girl," he said. "Haven't you city people heard of snow? Or did you just not know that it's cold?"

Half a dozen comebacks rose to Sylvia's lips, but as she sank into sleep, she couldn't make them move to form any of them.

Twenty-One

IT TOOK BETH A moment to recognize the smell that was wafting up the stairs as she came down them, but when she did, she smiled.

"Waffles," she said, when she stepped into the kitchen.

She had steeled herself on the way down to stay steady if she had to come face-to-face with Gloria first thing that morning, but with relief she saw only three faces there: Mitzi, who was whipping butter in a ceramic bowl, her mother at the stove, and Uncle Charlie at the table, already digging into a pile of her mother's fluffy breakfast creations.

"You see?" he said, twisting back to look at her mother. "I told you we should have saved some for the bride."

"She'll have her own in a minute," Beth's mother said, watching the timer on the old iron waffle maker run down. "If you survive yours."

"I told her I couldn't have the first helping," Uncle Charlie said, with a grin at Beth. "She said not to think of it as the first helping. I'm more like the taster for the king."

The timer on the waffle maker dinged. Beth's mother flicked a crusty golden waffle out of the greased metal grid, onto a plate, and laid the plate in front of Beth just as she took a seat beside Uncle Charlie.

"See?" Beth's mother said to him. "No one had to wait for anything."

"Thanks, Mom," Beth said. "But didn't Jen take care of breakfast? You weren't supposed to have to do this."

"Oh, she sent over a box of pastries," Beth's mother said. "I put them in the pantry."

She came over to Beth, leaned down to envelop her in a hug, then kissed her on the cheek. "I wanted to do this," she said.

Then she straightened up. "Plus, you're getting married today," she said. "You need something that will stick to your ribs more than a bit of pastry. Isn't that right?" she said, looking to Uncle Charlie for support.

Uncle Charlie leaned back and shook his head ruefully. "I wouldn't know," he said. "I've never been married."

Mitzi, who had finished whipping the butter, set it down beside Beth's plate and gave Uncle Charlie a look as if he were a frog who'd just belted out a line from a Broadway play. "Never married?" she repeated.

Uncle Charlie shrugged and smiled, but Beth thought she still saw a trace of sadness in his eyes as he ducked his head, which made her heart tug for him. Gloria had given her all kinds of warnings before she met Uncle Charlie, about what a disaster she expected him to be, but Beth had always liked him.

"I was kind of a mess as a young man," Uncle Charlie said. He smiled ruefully. "And then I was kind of a mess even when I wasn't young." He sighed.

"I don't see a trace of mess in your sister," Mitzi observed tartly.

Uncle Charlie took a deep breath. "We had a lot of . . . mess," he said. "Growing up. And I think we kind of handled it in opposite ways."

"I guess so," Mitzi said, with a significant look. It was obvious that she was making a comparison between the two of them, and that it wasn't favorable to Gloria.

But Uncle Charlie shook his head. "There were a lot of years," he said, "when Gloria was the only person in the world who was still willing to talk to me when I called. I put her through a lot."

"It sounds like you went through a lot," Nadine said, sitting down at the table with a waffle of her own, and a plate for Mitzi, too.

"I can tell you one thing for sure," Uncle Charlie said. "It's a very good thing I didn't manage to marry anybody back then. But still, sometimes, I regret it."

"Well," Beth's mother said lightly. "It's never too late."

At this, Beth saw, Uncle Charlie's whole countenance changed. It was if the thought had never actually occurred to him. He looked at Beth's mother with a totally open, hopeful expression, like a child who'd just been told that there was an extra bag of presents waiting in another room for him, after he thought he'd already opened up everything under the tree.

But quickly, he tried to hide it under his familiar expression of calm detachment. "Hmmph," he said, and added more syrup to his waffle, which was already drowning in it.

As Beth waited for him to finish so she could retrieve whatever remained of the syrup for her own waffle, her phone began to vibrate.

"Hello?" she said, checking the photo as she answered. "Veronica?"

"Beth," Veronica's voice crackled through the snow that was still falling outside. "I'm so sorry."

"Sorry?" Beth repeated. "For what?"

At this, all the heads around the table swiveled toward her. Beth waved at them to let them know not to worry, then rose from her seat.

Veronica was an old high school friend who had done both Beth and Destiny's hair for all their dances and proms. Now she ran the only salon in town, which had just opened up in the second-floor apartment over the drugstore that had held down one corner of Main Street since it was cool to get sodas after school at the drugstore lunch counter, which the old-fashioned store still boasted. And she was scheduled to arrive within the hour to do the girls' hair for the wedding that day.

"We're snowed in," Veronica said.

"You are?" Beth said, her voice rising in alarm and surprise.

Everyone at the table turned to look at her.

"Doesn't Dan have a truck?" Beth asked. Veronica had married the star linebacker of their football team, who had had a serious pickup even back in high school.

"He does," Veronica said. "But even his four-by-four can't get past the tree that's down over our road. We've got branches all the way up and down the drive. He got me about a quarter of a mile down it. Had to get out to pull off a couple of branches. But there's a big one down about halfway to our property line. The wind was too much for it. The whole crown is down in the middle of the drive. I know it's your wedding, sweetie. I'm so sorry I can't get there."

"I understand," Beth said. "Don't worry." The last thing she wanted at this wedding was to turn into some kind of bridezilla. And she wasn't angry at Veronica, or the world, because Veronica couldn't make it. But at the news that this piece of the wedding was going wrong, she felt a hard knot of dread begin to form in her stomach, and a host of doubts begin to flap around in her mind like bats. Even as she tried to tell herself it was just a little bump in the road, that it was to be expected, some other part of her was shouting that this was only the tip of the iceberg, that something was deeply wrong with the whole project, that she should run for the hills while she still could.

"Okay, love you," Veronica said. "We'll be praying for you from here. If there was anything I could do to get there, I'd do it."

"I know," Beth said. "Love you."

"Honey," Beth's mother said when she hung up. "What's wrong?"

"It's Veronica," Beth said. "She's snowed in." She was surprised by the tears that rose in her throat as she said it, but she managed to get through the sentence without her voice breaking.

"She a good friend of yours?" Uncle Charlie asked, clearly trying to understand the emotion he could see in her eyes.

And for some reason, his kindness undid Beth. "She was supposed to do my hair," she said. Even as she said it, she knew it was just a small thing. In the grand scheme, it couldn't matter much how her hair was done on this one day. It wouldn't affect her marriage, or the world—unless she let it.

But knowing that didn't keep two large tears from sliding down her face as her voice cracked.

Uncle Charlie looked away, embarrassed.

Even Mitzi bit her lip, holding back the tart comment Beth knew was somewhere on her tongue—probably something along the lines of, *Back in my day, we felt lucky just to have* hair.

Beth's mother took her hand. "You know what?" she said. "Maybe I could help you with it."

Beth looked into her mom's eyes and felt a wave of comfort. "You need to get ready, too," she said.

"I know," her mother said. "But it's early yet."

"Okay," Beth said.

"You going to finish your waffle?" Mitzi asked as Beth's mother rose from the table.

But Beth's mom was already leading her toward the stairs, her arm around Beth's waist.

When Beth sank down on her bed, her mother gently let Beth's partly wet hair down from the twist she'd turned it up in before coming downstairs.

"Your hair's so pretty anyway," her mother said. "We hardly need to do anything to it."

Beth didn't feel that way, but she was comforted by the feel of her mother's fingers as they untangled the loose knot.

A moment later, her mother had discovered her ancient high school hair dryer and was chasing the last dampness out.

When she set that aside, she picked up a comb.

Beth raised her hand. "It's better if you leave it a little messy to start," she said. "It gives it more volume."

"I know," her mother said. "But let me do this."

Suddenly, Beth knew exactly what her mother meant. Her mother wasn't just thinking back to all the times when she'd combed the tangles out of Beth's locks as a child. For as long as Beth could remember, her father had combed out her mother's hair every night. He'd done it when she was a tiny child, and he'd done it until he was too sick to raise the comb himself.

As her mother ran the comb gently through Beth's hair, Beth could almost feel him there with her, his love for both her mother and for her passing into Beth's worried heart, with every repetition of that simple action.

And, somehow, that love gave her hope. And that hope made her stubborn.

Her tears, and the dread she'd been fighting off that morning, had never been just about the details of the wedding: who would do her hair, what it would look like, which guests would and wouldn't be there. Her worries were about so much more: what it really meant to be a family, and what kind of family she wanted to be part of.

And suddenly she knew exactly what she had to do—about all of it.

Twenty-Two

"ARE YOU READY FOR this?" Jen asked, pasting a big smile on her face.

She had hoped she was going to be able to make it through her own kitchen, and out the door to the barn, without seeing anyone. So for the first time in her life, she'd been taken aback to smell the unmistakable scent of her father's buckwheat pancakes wafting out of the kitchen when she approached it from the hall, and hear the sizzle of what was almost certainly her father's own special-recipe breakfast sausage.

And when she'd walked in the kitchen, she'd discovered it wasn't just her father. Tom was already there, tucking into a stack of flapjacks tall enough to feature in a maple syrup commercial. And even worse, there was Jared.

He had helped her into the wee hours the night before, tying evergreens into the half-ruined flower arrangements with surprising dexterity. And after her long silence about his questions about whether she was happy, he'd lapsed back into a friendly chatter as they'd worked.

But that hadn't kept Jen from dreaming about him during the night. They weren't even romantic dreams, particularly, although they had brought up some of the sweet moments she remembered between them. Instead, they were just dreams of daily life where he was there, just there, as if he always had been.

It seemed so natural and so good—and so real—to have him there that she had woken up with a serious pang to remember that in this life, he still lived what might as well be a million miles away.

Tom grinned in reply to Jen's smile. "I think I've been ready for this since the day I met Beth," he said.

Jared gave Jen a questioning glance, but she let her eyes slide past him, out toward the barn. If she could just get her coat and boots, and—

But before she could pass by the high table in the middle of the kitchen where her family actually ate most of their meals, her mother plunked a plate of flapjacks down on the table in front of her with a big smile of pride.

"Oh, Mom," Jen said. "Thank you so much. But—"

"You've got to eat something," her mother said, in a tone that, even today, Jen knew was going to be fruitless to argue with.

Reluctantly, Jen plunked herself down at the table and began to motor through the flapjacks as her mother watched with pro-prietary interest.

After the first bite, she had to admit that her father had out-done himself. They were made of her father's hearty buckwheat base, but she'd added chopped apricots, walnuts, and . . . "Are these chocolate chips?" Jen asked.

She'd begged and begged for chocolate chips in her pancakes as a kid, and always received the curt answer that "Breakfast isn't dessert."

Her mother grinned at her, then nodded at Jen's father, who was finishing a cup of coffee by the sink, where a new set of fuzzy white angels had appeared on the windowsill, seemingly overnight—maybe her mother's way of celebrating the special day. "It was his idea," Jen's mother said.

"I didn't want these city folk to think that all we had to eat out here were bagels from a box," her father said.

Jen raised her eyebrows. The "bagels from a box" in question were actually from a Detroit bakery and excellent. She'd had boxes of them dropped off at the Fitzgeralds', and at the bed-and-breakfast in town where several of the other guests were staying.

But the most important detail, she realized, wasn't her dad's little dig at the citified breakfast she had tried to offer the guests, or the presence or absence of chocolate chips in the flapjacks. It was the fact that he had apparently developed enough pride in this whole crazy process of hosting a wedding in his barn that he had decided to trot out his ancestral pancakes to impress their out-of-town guests.

And the guests were duly impressed.

"These are delicious," Tom said, reaching over to give himself another generous helping of butter from the tureen on the table. "I've never had anything like them."

"That's Blue Hill butter," Jen's father informed him. "Got it from the Timerlys, down the road."

"Amazing," Tom said.

Jen's father looked over her shoulder to make sure she was making what he deemed to be appropriate progress on her stack of pancakes. She slid her arm around his waist to give her a squeeze. "Thanks, Dad," she said.

"Don't thank me," her father said gruffly. "You've got things to do. Eat!"

A few bites later, Jen had done what she judged to be sufficient damage to the stack, which there was no way in the world she could ever finish.

"This was delicious, Dad," she said. "But I've got to go check a few things in the barn."

"I'll go with you," Jared said, scrambling off his chair.

"You're not done," Jen's father protested, in a tone of voice that made Jen slightly nervous that he was about to address Jared, as he often had in the past, as "young man."

Well, she thought, suppressing a grin of amusement, it wouldn't be the worst thing in the world if Jared got a little rebuke from her dad. And if her dad could keep Jared from coming with her, more power to him. She didn't really know how she was going to deal with Jared, on top of everything else, today.

"I'm all right," she said. "Go ahead and finish up."

"Naw," Jared said, yanking on a pair of boots in the pile by the door as she fished her own out and pulled on a hat and coat. "I'm ready to go."

Jen couldn't figure out another way to put him off, so she just gave her father a kiss, waved to Tom, and dove out the back door, hoping that maybe, somehow, she'd lose Jared along the way, or at least get so absorbed in the tasks of the day that he didn't seem like such a distraction.

Outside, the world looked like a Christmas card.

Not one set of human tracks crossed the yard, perhaps because the storm in the night had dropped a blanket at least a good foot and a half deep over everything. Even the tracks she and Jared must have made coming back from the barn not so long ago were lost now in the drifts and new snowfall, crossed here and there only by the footprints of birds, and a few loping paw prints that might be a fox or just a stray dog.

Behind her on the porch, Jared let out a long sigh of appreciation. "It's beautiful," he said. "I haven't seen snow like this in so long."

"Most people wouldn't miss the snow," Jen said.

"I miss a lot of things," Jared said.

At that, Jen dove off, down the steps, which she could barely see below the humps of snow that showed their silhouettes, down to the yard. Part of her was annoyed. Jared obviously thought he had something he wanted to say to her, and he obviously thought that this was the time—after all these years, and in the middle of one of the biggest days of her own life.

But part of her was scared. She had ideas about what he might be trying to get around to saying. But was it just wishful thinking on her part? Was she the one who was still stuck back in the past, and not him? Would she be disappointed yet again by whatever it was he had to say? And what if he really did want to talk with her about them, about any feelings he might still have for her? What about her and Ed? What about all the years that had passed, and all the ways both she and Jared had grown since they were together before? Would it even work if they tried again? Because it hadn't last time. If he brought all that up, what would she say?

Jared plowed gamely along behind her, following her tracks as she blazed the familiar trail through the snow to the barn.

"How in the world are guests going to get through all this in their nice clothes?" Jared asked.

"I've got kids from down the road coming," Jen said. "They're going to shovel both drives, and make a path out to the barn. Then I've got a bunch of those industrial entryway rugs to cover the path from the drive to the barn. And some potted pine with lights to line them."

"Sounds pretty," Jared said.

They were almost to the barn now, and Jen calculated that she only had to get a few more steps before she could get inside. And once she was inside, she wouldn't be stuck with just him.

She could find some kind of task to bury herself in and tell him that they'd have to talk some other time, after the wedding. Or never. Never also seemed like a good option.

But before she could get there, Jared actually executed the heroic feat of striking out onto his own path on the snow, not just following the one she was forging for the two of them. He waded out into the snow up to his knees, and still managed to catch up to her and actually circle around a bit, driving her slightly off course on her way to the barn, as if she were a young filly he was trying to corral back to the herd.

"Hey, Jen," he said. "There was something I wanted to talk with you about."

"Mmph," Jen said, ducking her head and continuing doggedly on her way to the main doors.

"Yeah," Jared said. "I mean, I'd been thinking about this a lot, even before I got here, and then, after last night—"

"Can we talk about this some other time?" Jen asked, adding silently, *Or never?*

Jared shook his head and planted his feet in the snow. "Just—" he said. "Just let me. It's already been too long."

Jen sighed and crossed her arms.

"I never wanted to leave you," Jared said.

Jen raised her eyebrows.

Jared nodded, seeing her skepticism, and spread his hands. "But we were just kids," he said. "You know I always wanted to get out of this town, at least for a while. But I was scared to death. I never had a serious job before. I didn't know if they were going to fire me the first week I got down there. And I didn't . . ."

"Didn't what?" Jen asked.

"I didn't want you to see me fail," Jared said. "I could handle that with anyone else. But with you, it meant too much. Because

I care about what you think more than anyone else in the world."

Some part of Jen recognized that he'd just said "care" instead of "cared," as if it was still true.

But another part of her suddenly felt all the sorrow and pain from all those years ago. Her lips tightened and her eyes narrowed. "Well, you didn't give me any choice, did you?" Jen asked.

"I didn't think it was fair to ask you," Jared said. "I didn't want to put you in that position. And you didn't seem like . . ."

"What?" Jen demanded when he trailed off.

"You didn't seem like you cared that much," Jared said.

"Well, I wasn't going to beg you to stay," Jen said. "If you wanted to go. And," she added, in a quieter voice, "if you didn't want to be with me."

"Not be with you?" Jared said. "I never said that. I never—"

"You didn't have to," Jen said. "That was perfectly clear, as soon as you told me you wanted to leave, and you weren't planning on taking me."

"But how could I ask you to do that?" Jared asked. "Leave behind everything you know, and go someplace you'd never been, where you didn't have a job, just to be with me?"

"That would have been easy," Jen said.

"Easy?" Jared repeated. "How?"

Jen couldn't believe she even had to say it. "If we were married," she told him, exasperated.

It hadn't seemed possible, because they were already so wide, but Jared's eyes seemed to double in size.

"You would have *married* me?" he asked. "When I had *nothing*?"

The answer to that question was so clear in Jen's mind, and such a surprise to Jared, that she could feel tears springing to her eyes. To fight them back, she glanced away, at the barn. When she did, her eyes widened in shock.

Jared turned to see what she was looking at.

When he did, his own eyes widened.

"Wait," he said. "Did we—?"

"No," Jen said, diving for the barn door, which stood slightly open. "I did. I was the last one out, remember? I must not have— Did you see me . . . ?"

"It's okay," Jared said. But his tone sounded more like panicked babbling than comforting advice. "It's okay. Look, it's mostly shut. I bet it's fine."

By now, Jen had actually gotten to the door. She couldn't swing it open, because there was so much snow drifted up against the exterior of the barn. Together, she and Jared kicked and scrabbled at the snow until the door swung wide.

Then they stepped inside.

It didn't look like it had snowed as much inside the barn as it did outside. Outside, there were a good two feet of snow on the ground. Inside, there were only six inches.

But it was on everything.

The arbor at the front of the main aisle was dusted with fresh snow. Neat drifts sat on the seat of every chair, and nestled in between the fronds and needles of all the evergreen she and Jared had spent so long placing on the ends of chairs last night. And the entire floor of the barn, from the doorway all the way to the opposite side, was covered with snow: close to a foot of it at the door itself, where it had first blown in, then trickling off to a dusting on the far side. But there was no place in the entire place that hadn't been touched by Old Man Winter.

"I'll go get everyone," Jared said, turning for the door. "We're gonna need help."

"No!" Jen hissed, clutching his arm fiercely. "We will not get *anyone*. The very first job of a wedding planner is to make sure that the bride and groom and the families have no worries on their big day."

"And this," Jared said, looking around to take in the extent of the carnage, "would be a worry."

Jen nodded. "That's right. And there's practically no one here who isn't family."

"I bet Mitzi could make short work of this, though," Jared said, cracking a grin at his own joke.

Knowing Mitzi, Jen half believed him. But the disaster around her was so huge that she couldn't bring herself to smile.

"Okay," Jared said, in a tone that made it clear he wasn't absolutely sure it would be. "I'll go get a shovel. We can clean this up."

Jen looked around the place, calculating. Yes, you could shovel the place out—if you had ten men and a couple of hours. But even if they got the bulk of the snow out, how could they hold a wedding in the place? One of the first tasks on her list that morning had been to fire up the heaters that were meant to turn the place into a toasty refuge from the elements. If they fired them up now, the place would turn into a water park. And even once they got most of the snow out, any that was left would turn into ruinous water as soon as the temperature came up, spotting all the ribbon and chairs and decorations.

Not to mention the fact that she did not have anything like ten men at her disposal.

"The shovels are in here," Jen said, jamming the door back so that she could tramp through the drift at the threshold.

A minute later, they both had shovels in hand. Jared started tossing giant shovelfuls out the open door, but Jen grabbed a nearby wheelbarrow and took it down the aisle. If she started from this side, maybe they could meet in the middle. And if she could get most of the snow into wheelbarrow loads, maybe they could use a snowblower to blast away the rest of the flakes that might be left on anything that would be ruined when the flakes melted.

Her mind raced, calculating how quickly they could clear the place—and if that would be quick enough to get it into order in time for the guests to arrive.

Then her thoughts were interrupted by the ringing of a phone.

Her heart stopped. What in the world would she tell Beth if it turned out to be her calling? She couldn't bear the idea of lying to Beth on her wedding day. And she couldn't think of any way to tell her this particular truth.

But when she pulled the phone out, it was Ed's face on the screen. Before she thought twice, she answered it.

"Hey!" Ed boomed cheerfully. "You all ready for the big day?"

Jen looked around at the barn that she'd worked so hard to turn into a wedding hall, and that the snow had reclaimed in a few short hours.

"No," she said flatly, without any attempt to cushion the news.

"What?" Ed yelped in surprise. "Honey! What's wrong? What's going on?"

"The barn door came open," Jen said. "The whole place is full of snow."

"Honey," Ed said. "I'll be there as soon as I can."

More help was exactly what Jen needed, but when she thought of Ed being there, her heart sank. Part of it was that he lived so far out of town that there was a good chance they'd have the place cleaned up by the time he could fight through the snowbound roads to get there. If they didn't have the place cleaned up, and heating, in about an hour, there might not be a wedding at all. But that wasn't really it, she suddenly realized with a blinding flash. Even if Ed could get there that very instant, she didn't really want him there. He'd be so busy trying to take care of her, and prove how much he cared about her, that he might not be much help at all.

"No," Jen said. "It'll take you too long. I think we can take care of it."

"'We'?" Ed asked, his voice turning quiet.

Jen felt impatience rising in her heart at the thought of having to spare his feelings when she was in the midst of her own disaster. "Jared's here," she said shortly. "He's helping me deal with it."

"Jared, huh?" Ed said.

"I'm sorry," Jen said. "Things are a mess here. I really have to go."

With a twist in her heart, she hung up the phone.

But before she could even grab the handles of the wheelbarrow again, she was distracted by a flicker in the light at the barn door.

It hadn't even occurred to her to worry about anyone else stumbling into this mess, but apparently somebody already had.

And as her eyes adjusted to the light, she recognized who the couple must be from the fine lines of their silhouettes, and the cluster of fur at the woman's throat: Ken and Gloria Allerton. The last people in the world she wanted to see right now—or who she wanted to have to see the disaster she was currently standing in the midst of.

Her heart in her throat, Jen walked down the long aisle to meet them, a new smile pasted on her face.

"Morning!" Ken called heartily. "We just thought we'd take a little walk. Don't let us get in your way."

"What an amazing effect you've gotten," Gloria said as Jen arrived to greet them. "It almost looks like real snow."

Jen came to a stop in front of them, too dumbfounded to even try to think of a way to spin the situation. "That's because it is," she said.

Twenty-Three

WHEN SYLVIA WOKE UP, in the first moments before she opened her eyes, the first thing she felt was the comfort of a steady warmth emanating from someplace nearby. Scrambling for its footing, her mind cast around for some explanation of what in the world this could be, and took her all the way back to her childhood, when her mother had sometimes warmed her clothes for her on the noisy radiator that sounded like it was being hammered from within by mischievous elves, all night long.

Then, with a whirl that seemed to spin the whole world around a couple times before it put her down, she came back to the present moment, and looked around.

She was still bundled under a pile of blankets, and the warmth she had felt glowed from the big black stove Winston had settled her beside when he brought her in. But the room was bigger than she had remembered: a wide great room that ran all the way from the front of the house to the back windows, where a kitchen looked out over more endless white fields. A set of stairs led up to the second floor from the entryway off the front door. And the large room she sat in was comfortably furnished with sturdy, old-fashioned furniture, including a remarkably beautiful wooden dining table, and a small Christmas tree decorated with what appeared to be a single strand of white lights, and what looked for all the world like little bows made out of the scraps of a plaid shirt.

At first, she thought she might even be alone, but then she spotted Winston, quietly reading, with his big feet in a pair of thick wool socks propped up on a nearby couch with a hand-braided scrap rug at his feet.

Before she could think of what to say, he noticed the movement in her direction, and looked up.

"How you doing, Sleeping Beauty?" he asked.

Suddenly, the question of how long she'd been sleeping rose to the surface of Sylvia's mind. "What time is it?" she asked, sitting upright so fast that the rocker she was sitting in whacked against the floor.

"Easy there," Winston said. He glanced at a large clock on the wall that looked to be several generations old, and advertised a brand of tobacco Sylvia had never heard of before.

When her eyes followed his, she relaxed. She felt as if she'd been out for days, but it hadn't even been an hour.

"You haven't been here for long," Winston told her. "I wasn't about to let you miss Beth's wedding."

"Thank you," Sylvia said as Winston stood.

"You want a cup of coffee?" Winston asked. "To warm up a bit before I take you back?"

Sylvia couldn't even begin to imagine what passed for coffee this far from civilization, but she also wasn't about to turn her nose up at Winston's kindness, given what he'd just done for her.

"Thank you," she said again, then stood and wrapped a blanket around herself, padding after Winston as he began to rummage around in the kitchen.

But between her chair and the kitchen, she stopped, captured by the simple beauty of the large dining table. It had been fastened with wood pegs, not nails or screws, and it managed to be massive and sophisticated at the same time, with substantial weight and a simple but arresting design, all stained a beautiful shade of sorrel, a vibrant orange red somewhere between the standard blond or mahogany stains of most industrial woods.

"This is beautiful," she said. "Has it been in your family a long time?"

Winston, who had been pouring water directly from the tap into an open pan, placed the pan on the stovetop, fired up a gas burner, and turned back.

"Since last year," he said.

"Last year?" Sylvia repeated.

Winston nodded, then lost the battle with the grin he'd been holding back. "When I made it," he said.

"You *made* this?" Sylvia asked. She knelt down to get a closer look at the table, which was even more beautiful the more she looked—the grain of the wood dense and lovely, the matte varnish saturated without being showy.

"Yep," Winston said. "I mean, I made some of these other little pieces around here, too. But this was the first real big one."

"Which ones?" Sylvia asked. Before he could answer, her gaze landed on an end table, about three feet in diameter, made from a crosscut of a large tree trunk. The bark of the trunk had been stabilized with glue but otherwise left untouched, but the rings of the trunk had been sealed and varnished to a high gloss. "This?" she asked.

Winston nodded. "That was my first," he said. "I took down this tree, and I couldn't get over those rings. It's two hundred and fifty-three years old."

"You counted them all?" Sylvia asked.

"I spent a lot of time with it," Winston said simply.

"What kind of tree is it?" Sylvia asked.

"Elm," Winston said. "They're real rare around here. Had a

disease back after World War II, knocked them all out. But somehow this one lasted—at least till now. I had to take it down because it was starting to rot out at the top, and it was too near a house. But when I made that cut at the bottom, it was solid as a rock."

"And this?" Sylvia asked, pointing to a two-person bench sitting alongside the big black stove. Its seat wasn't polished like the others, just sanded soft, the natural curves at the edge of the wood left as rounded edges, rather than blunted off into square corners. But the wood itself was dark and the grain was fine.

"That's walnut," Winston said. "I hated to take that tree down, but it was dropping a couple thousand nuts in the yard every year, and it was an older couple. So it just got to be too much for them."

"Do you make something out of every tree you take down?" Sylvia asked.

Winston shook his head. "I wish," he said. "But that'd be its own whole business. I take down a lot of trees."

"The table's so much bigger than these others," Sylvia said, returning to the large piece that had caught her eye in the first place.

Winston ducked his head.

"Yeah," he said.

Sylvia looked at him closely.

"Was it a special tree?" she asked.

"I guess you could say that," Winston said. He looked up and met her eyes. "Maybe it was more like a special time."

Something in Sylvia told her to just be quiet as Winston came over to the table and ran his hand over the smooth surface himself.

"I made it after my dad died," he said finally, almost as if he was talking to the wood under his hand, and not to her.

"Hm," Sylvia said, to let him know she was listening, without interrupting anything else he might want to add.

"He was always going to teach me how to make a table," Winston said. "You should have seen the one we had before this. I broke our old table wrestling around with a friend, and we just brought in the picnic table from out back and used it in here. For years."

He smiled at the thought, then shook his head. "Dad was always saying that he was going to make me make a table after I turned eighteen. Something about being a real man, you know, making your own table."

Sylvia had no idea, actually. She didn't know a single man in New York who had ever given a thought to the idea that he could make a stick of his own furniture. But she knew better than to say that. At least not this instant.

"Then one day . . ." Winston snapped his fingers. "Heart attack," he said.

Suddenly, Sylvia realized why he had been so steady with her the night before, when the loss of her own mom had come up. It was because he knew what it was like. He'd been through it before. And he'd lost both parents—not just his mom.

"I'm sorry," Sylvia said quietly.

Winston shrugged. Like her, she suspected, the loss was too big to dredge up every time someone stumbled across it in conversation. And that wasn't the central part of the story he was trying to tell her now.

"It was real quiet out here," Winston said. "After that." For a moment, he lapsed into silence himself, as if giving her a taste of what it had been like in the house in those days.

"TV," he said with a shrug. "Radio, it didn't help. I knew I needed to actually do something. And I kept thinking how he always wanted me to build a table. So I thought, *I'll build a table*."

"It's beautiful," Sylvia said.

"It didn't start that way," Winston said with a grin. "In fact, I took it apart and replaced so many pieces that this might be more like the third or fourth table I built, when you come right down to it. But when I was done, I knew how to build a table."

The pride on his face was unmistakable. But so, to Sylvia's eyes, was the trace of loss.

"It sounds like your dad did teach you how to build a table, after all," she said quietly.

Winston's eyes widened. Then he looked away quickly, blinking. It took him a minute to collect himself, but then he met her eyes again. "I never said that to anyone before," he said. "But you know, that's always kind of how I think about it."

He glanced around the room, then perked his ear toward the stove, where the pot of water had started to boil.

"Hang on," he said, and rattled around a bit in the kitchen, picking up various dishes and implements. She expected him to douse a tablespoon of instant coffee in the tap water and hand it to her, but to her surprise, he continued rummaging around, pouring and adjusting for several minutes, as the aroma of delicious coffee filled the whole place, before he turned back and offered her a large mug.

Experimentally, Sylvia sniffed it, then took a sip. The taste was some of the best coffee she'd ever had: fruity, fresh, with just the right amount of bite in the bitterness.

Her eyes widened. "Where did you get this?" she asked.

"I've got a friend who knows I like coffee," Winston said. "He works in Detroit and brings it back for me. There's this farm-to-table coffee place downtown, gets these beans that were on the tree down in Colombia like sometime last week."

"It's delicious," Sylvia said.

Winston's grin turned wicked. "And you were complaining I wouldn't take you to Starbucks," he said.

Sylvia shook her head and rolled her eyes back at him. "Nobody had told me what the local options were," she said.

"You didn't seem real interested in hearing about them," Winston shot back.

"Well," Sylvia said, giving a decisive knock to the table to change the subject, since she knew she was losing this little argument. "If you ever wanted another business, you could have one, making this stuff."

"Naw," Winston said, in a tone of disbelief so thick it bordered on derision.

"You could," Sylvia insisted. "People would pay a lot for this stuff in the city."

"Only problem with that," Winston said, still grinning, "is that then I'd have to go to the city."

Sylvia raised her eyebrows. "I was thinking that might give you a chance to visit your friends there," she said.

Winston laughed. "I've only got one friend in the city," he said. "And that's Beth."

"Oh, I don't know," Sylvia said. "I'd say you've got more than that."

Winston looked at her with surprise. Then, as he started to catch her drift, he smiled. "Well," he said, raising his own eyebrows. "That's the only reason I could ever think of that might make me want to visit."

Twenty-Four

"NOW WHERE DO YOU think you're going?" Mitzi asked.

Halfway across the kitchen, Beth froze as if she were still a six-year-old and her grandmother had just caught her sneaking across the tile to get one more cookie in the middle of the night.

Before she stepped into the room, she had given it a once-over to make sure the coast was clear. But apparently Mitzi had been rummaging around in the pantry behind the fridge, which screened the pantry completely from the rest of the room. And when Beth had made it halfway across the tile, her grandmother popped up, seemingly out of thin air, like a fairy godmother arriving at the absolute most inopportune moment.

"Um," Beth said.

Mitzi glanced skeptically at Beth's head, which was currently wrapped in a bright emerald-and-pink scarf, one of her childhood treasures, which her mother had wrapped her updo in, after pin-curling the tendrils that she ultimately planned to leave loose and curly.

"Don't tell me this is some New York wedding fashion," Mitzi said. "You know, a whole lot of foolishness has come out of that place."

"Don't worry," Beth said with a smile, patting the scarf and the beautiful coils and twists her mother had created under it. "This won't make it down the aisle."

But Mitzi was still planted between Beth and the door. And she cocked her eyebrow to make it clear that Beth still hadn't answered her original question: Where was Beth off to?

"Um," Beth said again, edging past Mitzi to collect her father's boots, which were still standing by the door, because no one had had the heart to give them away. For years, her father's boots had been her favorite choice to slip on when she had to make a quick run into the snow. And although she'd wished before that her mother would just let go of so many of the reminders of him that littered the whole house, she now felt a little surge of warmth and gratitude that these familiar things were right where they had always been. "I've just got to go out for a minute."

"What do you need?" Mitzi demanded, with a disapproving glance up the stairs. "Can't you get one of those bridesmaids to do it for you? Don't those New York girls know they've got work to do?"

Beth wondered briefly where in the world Sylvia was, anyway. But this wasn't some simple chore that Sylvia could do for her, in any case. And the longer she waited, the more complicated it was going to get.

"I'm just going to run over to Jen's to do something."

"Jen can't do it?" Mitzi asked. "Don't you two have telephones?"

Beth smiled and sighed. "Jen can't do it, Grandma," she said. "I have to talk with Tom."

She braced herself, waiting for the inevitable barrage of traditionalist disapproval: a long list of reasons why it was bad luck for the bride to see the groom before the wedding, probably embellished with lurid tales of disasters suffered by couples who had been foolish or unlucky enough to break the ban.

But instead, Mitzi just lifted her chin. "You need to talk to him, eh?" she said, giving Beth a searching look.

"Yeah, Grandma," Beth said. "I do."

"Well," Mitzi said, giving a decisive nod. "Then you go over there and talk to him. And make sure you tell him *everything*."

Beth smiled in surprise.

Mitzi reached up to pinch Beth's cheek, which still hurt just as much as it had when Beth was a kid. As Beth reached up to comfort the spot, which continued to sting, Mitzi's face broke out in a wide grin. "And you keep telling him everything," she said with a determined look. "Even after you're married. You hear me?"

"I hear you, Grandma," Jen said. She gave Mitzi a peck on the cheek, then pulled on a coat from the jumbled collection of work jackets hanging on the coat hooks beside the door.

"You tell him!" Mitzi called after her as Beth slipped out the door and tromped down the thick snow of the back porch.

Over at Jen's place, Beth could see Mr. Fitzgerald in the yard, tossing snow this way and that with the help of a giant silver shovel, to clear the drive and the paths that ran between the house and barn.

But aside from a single set of prints leading down the back steps, the snow in the Dean yard was unspoiled. It had been so long since Beth had seen a wide field of white anywhere in the city, where the snow almost always melted immediately from the stored heat of the city streets, or turned into a gray slush even when it did stick around for any considerable amount of time, that the sight took Beth back to her childhood thrill at the sight of a first snowfall.

She leapt down the steps, two at a time, until she hit the fresh drifts of the yard, where she waded happily through them, gasping with delight at the cold air in her lungs and the clouds of fresh powder that rose up from around her knees with every new step as she followed the path to the Fitzgerald house, which she knew by heart even though it was completely lost from sight now, under the piles of snow.

When she broke through the lilac hedge into the Fitzgerald yard, suddenly the path was cleared, with glimpses of the evergreen of the crabgrass that was waiting to wake up, matted together with the snow that had gotten packed down into the earth as Mr. Fitzgerald cleared away the rest of it.

At her appearance, Mr. Fitzgerald paused in his exertions, his face red, puffs of white bursting from his lips with each breath. "Well, good morning, Beth!" he called from a few steps away.

"Good morning, Mr. Fitzgerald," Beth said.

She tried to continue blithely on and up the Fitzgeralds' back steps, but it wasn't an easy trick to be blithe when she was also clodhopping through the snow in her father's old boots.

"Ah, Beth," Mr. Fitzgerald said, when she'd only gone a few steps. "You know, Tom's in there at breakfast."

There was no way to hide her intentions, so Beth decided the best way forward was just to be direct. "Good," she said. "I need to see him."

She could see Mr. Fitzgerald open his mouth to make the standard objection, but just as quickly as he did, he closed it again, then shook his head in a way that, without saying a word, conveyed both the fact that he believed city folk to be completely crazy, and quite a bit more than a trace of satisfaction over the fact that, once again, the city folk had proven him right by acting just as crazy as he'd always thought they were.

Before he could change his mind and mount another objection, Beth scurried by, caught the rail of the Fitzgeralds' back steps, and tromped up them.

She pulled off her dad's boots in the Fitzgeralds' glassed-in mudroom, then peered through the glass of the mudroom door into the kitchen. To her relief, Tom was there. And he was alone.

When she stepped in, she realized in a flash how she must look, wearing a wild-colored scarf, a khaki work coat with a dark brown corduroy collar, and socks. But before she could even open her mouth to explain, Tom broke into a big grin at the sight of her.

He got up and pushed his chair back in one swift movement, with the same delight in his eyes that he always had when he saw her. It was one of the things she loved about him most. She'd dated other guys who had come on strong in the beginning, then seemed to lose their enthusiasm, or even any interest in her at all, as their relationship dragged on. But with Tom, he always seemed genuinely as eager to see her as he ever had in their early days. And over the entire year-plus that they'd been together, even in the midst of some situations that had been a whole lot less than delightful, that had never changed.

Except now it did. Before she even said anything, the smile faded from his face into worry, and after taking a few steps toward her, he suddenly stopped in his tracks.

At first, Beth wondered if there was something wrong with her—the outfit, the weird scarf. But his expression wasn't just one of surprise or confusion. It was deepening into real fear.

That's when she realized Mr. Fitzgerald and her grandmother weren't the only traditionalists in the place. She and Tom had never intended to break the rule about the bride not seeing the groom before their wedding, either. So Tom knew that she would never have come over to talk to him on their wedding morning unless it was incredibly important. And from the look on his face, she could see that he was worried—deeply worried—about what she might have to say. Which only made sense, after the fight they'd had before the rehearsal last night.

As soon as she realized how much her arrival had unsettled Tom, Beth rushed over to him, nestled in his arms, and turned her face up for a kiss, which he gave her quickly and tenderly.

"I love you," she said.

"I love you," he replied, as he always did. But there was still a question in his eyes.

Beth took both his hands in hers and looked up at him. "That's what I came to tell you," she said.

Tom took a deep breath, still watching her closely, as if he knew there was more to it than that.

"I thought about it all night," Beth said. "And this morning, I realized I don't care what your mother thinks about us. I don't just want to marry you. I want to be part of your family. But the promises I'm making, I'm making them to you. And I'm not going to let anyone else get in the way of them."

"What she asked you isn't right," Tom said. "I never would have asked you to do that. And I'll tell her—"

Beth shook her head. "I know you would," she said. "But you don't have to. Because this isn't about her. That's what I came to tell you. It's about us. You asked me to marry you. I said yes. We're the ones who are going to join our lives and live together. I know in my heart, deep in my heart, that it's the right thing. The rightest thing I've ever known," she said.

She thought she saw Tom's eyes brighten with what might have been tears as she said this, but she went on. "And I'm not going to let anyone mess that up for us," she said. "I believe in your promises to me. And I hope you know you can believe in my promises to you."

"I do," Tom said.

Beth nodded. "Well, that's enough for me," she said. "And if it's enough for you, then I don't care what anyone else in the world thinks. Even your mom.

"I'm not going to let anyone stop me from marrying you," Beth said. "*And* enjoying the heck out of it. Because we've worked hard for this day. And the day doesn't even matter, compared to the whole life we're going to get to spend together. And I don't want to let anyone else steal any happiness from us, ever again. Is that a deal?"

This was a little joke between them, since Tom was always closing deals in real life—they made deals about everything from whether they'd have Thai or Turkish food for dinner, to how many people they'd invite to the wedding. But she'd never asked the question over anything this serious before.

"Deal," Tom said instantly.

"And one more thing," Beth said, as if she'd just remembered an important caveat to the whole arrangement.

Tom raised his eyebrows, listening.

"I love you," Beth said.

"You said that before," Tom said, cracking a grin.

As it always did, Tom's grin momentarily derailed Beth's train of thought. She kissed him.

"Mm," Tom said as their lips parted. "If it's bad luck to see each other before the ceremony, I bet it's even worse luck to kiss."

"Well, we've already tempted the bad luck," Beth said. "So I guess you better kiss me again."

Twenty-Five

"YEAH," JARED SAID ENTHUSIASTICALLY. "Look at that. It looks a lot better."

Standing under the snow-covered arbor at the front of what was supposed to be a wedding venue in a few short hours, Jen bit her lip to keep from crying—or yelling.

She wasn't sure what, exactly, Jared was enthusing about. In the half hour since she'd discovered the disaster in the barn, she'd managed to find three shovels and a pair of brooms, all of which were being used to fill an old wheelbarrow that they carted out the back door to dump out seemingly every three minutes without making any significant dent, that Jen could see anyway, in the quantity of snow that remained under the roof of the barn.

Maybe it was better in the sense that being buried up to your knees in sand was better than being buried up to your neck. But at this point, Jen hardly felt like she was skipping freely down a beach. Or anywhere near ready for a wedding.

The main aisle had been mostly cleared, but there was still snow in every other aisle—and still dozens of wheelbarrows' worth of snow piled up by the door, despite the full wheelbarrows they'd been carting away, one after another, in what felt like a never-ending procession.

That Greek mythological king who had been stuck pushing

a rock up a mountain again and again flashed in Jen's mind—not because he had it worse than her, but because at least he wasn't also freezing to death as he rolled his stone back up the hill again.

As she contemplated the carnage, Destiny came down the aisle with a broom, the only implement that had still been available when she showed up. *Bless her heart*, Jen thought. Her duties as a bridesmaid shouldn't have involved anything more than doing her hair and zipping Beth into her dress, and making sure neither of them had too many prewedding mimosas. But Destiny had made the mistake of poking her head into the barn on her way over to Beth's place, and when she'd seen what was at stake, she hadn't hesitated to dive in—a decision that had already had unfortunate consequences for her bridesmaid's dress, whose hem was now caked with snow and hanging unevenly around the snow boots she'd worn over in the car.

Still, Jen was grateful to see that, as Destiny swept her way down the first row of chairs, the snow dusted on them completely disappeared from the concrete block they'd been set up on. And Jen had already managed to sweep the seats of the chairs clean of snow themselves. It was one of the first things she'd done when she realized what had happened, to make sure that the chairs themselves would be usable if they could only get the rest of the barn into shape.

Maybe, Jen told herself, if they could just get the area around the seats clear of snow, everyone else would make the same mistake that Gloria had when she first came in, and just assume that the piles of white stuff still drifting in the corners were just an unusual, even quaint, Midwestern wedding decoration.

But even as she thought this, she knew every flake of snow they could get out of the place had to be swept or shoveled away. The instant they heated the place up to a livable temperature, every single one of those flakes would turn into a drop of water. If they hadn't managed to get most of it out, the place would turn into a soggy, humid, slippery mess. And if they wanted the temperature in the barn to be anything over fifty for the ceremony, they had to start firing up the heaters now. In fact, they should have been running for half an hour already—ever since she'd come out to the barn to turn them on, and realized what had gone on once the wind had blown the doors open and the storm had swept in.

But before Jen could build up a really good panic about how in the world they were ever going to get the barn up to temperature in time, the barn door creaked open behind her again. When she swung it open, there was Beth's mother, Nadine, with Uncle Charlie in tow. And when Nadine saw Jen's face, her own face turned to surprise and a kind of bashfulness, almost like a teenager who had gotten caught sneaking around with a boyfriend.

Jen looked from Uncle Charlie to Nadine and then back again, trying to make any sense at all of this new development—at the same time her mind was racing, trying to decide whether to chase them away from the scene of the disaster, or drag them in instantly and commandeer their help. Nadine was still wearing sensible farm clothes, not her mother-of-the-bride outfit. And Uncle Charlie was wearing what looked like a pair of Beth's dad's old boots.

"We don't want to be in the way, honey," Nadine said. "But Charlie wanted to see the barn all set up."

Before Jen could make the decision about whether to shoo them away or ask them for help, it was made for her when Gloria came wobbling down the aisle with the wheelbarrow and poked her head through the door.

"What are you two doing here?" she asked.

"Oh my goodness," Nadine said, pushing her way into the barn. Instantly, she took in what had happened. "The barn door . . ." she said as Jen nodded.

"Got another shovel?" Uncle Charlie asked gamely.

Jared, who had just come up, handed him one.

"Nadine," Jen said. "I'm so sorry about this."

But Nadine just gave a quick shake of her head, already glancing around the barn with a practiced eye. "We're going to take care of all this," she said. "Don't you worry."

An instant later, she had a broom in hand, sweeping up the fine grains of snow from between the feet of the chairs, as everyone else fell back into a working rhythm together.

Grateful, Jen glanced over at Gloria, trying to check her mood. When Gloria had realized what had really happened in the barn, she'd looked around the place with the air of someone who was looking for the nearest servant to summon. Jen had half expected her to start snapping her fingers at Jen herself. But when Jen had produced the shovels, Ken had taken one himself. And Gloria, when she saw the wheelbarrow getting knocked around with each thudding chunk of snow that Jared and Ken pitched into it, had grabbed on to stabilize it with surprising determination, and then, without anyone asking her to, noted when the wheelbarrow had gotten full, wheeled it down to the back of the barn herself, and wrestled the back door open to dump it out. Then she'd proceeded to repeat that whole procedure, load after load, without one complaint or sly remark—at least that Jen had heard.

But now, even though there were still dozens, if not hundreds, more loads of snow to go, Gloria was starting to look a little peaked. Her jaw was set and determined, but the front wheel of the wheelbarrow wobbled in her hands, and as she came down the main aisle, which was starting to get a little slick from the traffic, she slipped.

"Here," Destiny said. "Let me get that."

"I can—" Gloria began to protest, but Destiny politely but firmly took her place between the two long handles of the wheelbarrow and rolled it out the back door, where Jen could hear the *whoosh* of snow on snow as she dumped it out.

Jen glanced around the barn. Maybe, she thought, if they moved all the chairs, they could do a virtually perfect job of sweeping the concrete floor of the barn, and at least keep that section mostly dry, even when the heat came on. It would mean taking time to pull the chairs down and set them up again, but if they could keep at least one quadrant of the place warm and dry for the guests, it would be worth it.

She turned to ask Jared what he thought of the idea, but he wasn't where he'd been earlier, standing beside her at the head of the aisle. And he wasn't, she realized as she checked the rest of the barn, anywhere in sight.

As she realized this, Ken Allerton came up and laid a hand on his wife's shoulder. "You getting worn out?" he asked. "It's cold in here. Maybe you should go back to the house."

To Jen's surprise, Gloria responded by tossing her head and raising an eyebrow. "Of the two of us," she said, "I don't think you're exactly the expert in farm work."

Ken's own eyebrows rose up in surprise.

"I'm the one who picked peaches every summer, remember?" Gloria said. "You're the one who never did a lick of real work."

It was such a sharp response that Jen could barely bring herself to look at Ken, because she was worried that, on top of everything else, she was about to play host to a royal melee between the mother and father of the groom.

But when she finally did dare to look at Ken's face, it had broken out into a grin.

And even more surprising, Gloria was grinning back at him. Then she swiped the shovel from his hands as Destiny rolled by with the wheelbarrow.

From the other side of the barn, where he was helping Nadine load a small rolling cart full of snow, Charlie laughed. "She's got a point there, Ken," he said.

"I think maybe *you're* the one who needs a break," Gloria told her husband as she turned to follow Destiny. "Why don't you handle the wheelbarrow for a minute?" she called over her shoulder to Charlie.

Ken Allerton just stood there, shaking his head, looking after his wife with an expression that Jen realized, with another jolt of surprise, was admiration.

But before she could process what all that could mean, the far door of the barn opened—the one that led from the houses and the drive, where the guests and the rest of the family would come from.

As light poured in, turning the snow on the floor a dazzling, glimmering white, Jen's heart leapt to her mouth. It was still hours before the ceremony was to begin—but not that many hours. And one of the things her wedding planning books had emphasized was that when an event had as many guests as the average wedding, they could be wildly unpredictable, and hard to manage. You never wanted to be decorating or otherwise preparing until the last minute, several of the books advised. Because you could never be sure that Cousin Janet wasn't going to show up two hours early with her six kids.

But were people really showing up this early—in this weather? Jen wondered. And if they were, what in the world was she going to do with them? She could stash a few in the farm-houses, she guessed. But she hadn't done any cleaning or prep over there—and they were the staging grounds not just for all the members of the family to get ready, but for the caterers.

Before she could come to any conclusions, the door swung shut again, and as the bright sunlight winked out, her eyes adjusted enough to recognize Jared's familiar figure, wrestling with some kind of metal box.

Jen headed down the aisle to get a better look at it.

"Hey," Jared said, looking up with a grin when he heard her footsteps behind him. "Look what I found."

Jen looked quizzically at the contraption, which seemed to be a cross between a lawn mower and an air conditioner, and about fifty years old.

"What is it?" she asked.

Jared squinted up at her, grinning. "A snowblower," he said. "I found it in the Dean barn."

Jen looked down at the old machine, mildly bewildered. Snowblowers made sense in town, where people had acres of sidewalk and driveway to clear before they could get to work in the morning. But in the country, there were no sidewalks. Boots were de rigueur even on the sunniest day, so people were hardly worried about getting their shoes ruined. And virtually everyone had a 4x4 truck, which meant nobody needed to go to the trouble of clearing their own drives. For the life of her, she couldn't think of a single reason why Mr. Dean would have a snowblower stashed in his small barn.

"Why in the world did he have that?" she asked.

Jared shrugged.

"Dunno," he said. "It was in that little workshop in the corner. He had a couple toasters and a riding lawn mower back there, too. Maybe he was working on a time machine, and he needed them for parts."

That was about as reasonable an explanation as Jen could think of, herself.

Then Jared, who had been inspecting the old machine the whole time they were talking, stood up, flicked a switch, and began to yank a pull cord out of the body of the machine. In response, its engine flickered and coughed.

"Whoa, whoa," Jen said. "Wait a minute."

"What?" Jared said, his tone somewhere between exasperated and impatient. "Don't you want to clean this place out?"

Jen decided not to dignify this with a response. Instead, she resorted to facts. "It looks like nobody's used that thing in years," she said. "And if you start it up in here, it's going to blow snow everywhere."

"Exactly," Jared said. "At least, that's what we *hope* it'll do."

Jen shook her head impatiently.

"No," she said. "We need to get it *out* of here."

"If I can get this running," Jared said, "I can blow all the snow in this place over to the back wall. It might be a mess in the meantime, but it'll only take twenty minutes."

Jen hesitated, calculating.

"Have you got a better idea?" Jared asked.

Jen took a deep breath, then shook her head.

"All right," Jared said, and gave another gigantic yank to the machine's pull cord.

Jen looked down at it as it stuttered, thinking maybe the little argument with Jared had been moot because the thing would never start after all these years anyway. But as she watched, it shuddered, whirred, and then began to spit snow.

"Look at this!" Jared whooped, as a giant arc of snow began

to shoot from the metal mouth of the little machine, getting stronger as Jared pushed it forward.

Jen looked down at what had just been a pile of snow at her feet an instant before, her eyes widening at the prospect of what the machine could do. The area they were standing by, an untouched drift about a foot and a half high, was gone, leaving nothing but a few flakes that could easily be swept away by Destiny's broom.

And if Jared was careful about where he shot the vanquished snow, she thought, he could easily direct it all toward . . .

That's when she looked up to see exactly where the snow Jared was blowing now was going. And saw the thick arc of white leaping through the area, aimed directly at Gloria Allerton's perfectly coiffed head.

Jen leapt into a modified tackle, grabbing Jared around the waist and knocking him off balance, and the snowblower out of action.

But it was too late. As Jared reached for her, wrapping his arms around her to keep upright, the blast of snow connected with Gloria's head at exactly the same time the two of them were engaged in the awkward little shuffle of their own strange dance.

She thought she saw something strange in Jared's eyes when they met hers—a flare of hope, or even desire. But she didn't have time to deal with it at that moment.

Instead, she broke free of Jared's clumsy embrace, and barreled over toward Gloria, knocking away several of the gathered chairs in the process. After a few steps, she could hear Jared gasp behind her, and his footsteps following her.

When they reached Gloria, she was shaking a huge cloud of snowflakes out of her smooth blond hair.

"Oh my gosh," Jen said. "Mrs. Allerton. I'm so sorry. We didn't—"

"It was my fault," Jared broke in behind her. "I wasn't looking. I'm so, so sorry."

"Honey?" Ken Allerton was holding his wife by both shoulders, looking into her eyes, and scanning her for any injuries. "Are you all right?"

Uncle Charlie just guffawed, while Nadine tried her best to hide a smile.

To Jen's relief, she didn't see any cuts or even contusions—no signs or marks on Gloria's face, other than the snow starting to mat in her hair from the heat of her scalp. And after having clambered through the chairs to get to Gloria, Jen realized how far the snow had had to go—and how much it had probably slowed down on the way, so that whatever hit her was more like a pot of snow dumped over on her head than the snow-cannon blast that had come out of the mouth of the snowblower at the source. It didn't look to Jen like there was going to be any lasting damage. Or even any damage that would still be visible by the time the ceremony rolled around.

But that didn't, Jen understood deep in her bones, mean that Gloria would think she was fine.

The cold hand of dread clenching around her heart, Jen watched Gloria's face. As she did, Gloria pushed her hair back, wiped away the snowflakes that were starting to slide down it, and looked at Jared with a stern expression.

Jared took a wobbly step backward under the ferocity of her gaze, then took a deep breath and stepped forward again. "I don't have any excuse," he said. "I'm so sorry about that."

"Gloria," Ken Allerton said. "How do you feel? Does it hurt?"

Ignoring him, Gloria continued to stare at Jared with a gaze that looked for all the world as if she were a fearsome sea captain hesitating over the decision between putting him in the stocks or throwing him overboard.

Then suddenly she bent down, scrabbled in the snow at her feet, straightened up again, and landed a giant snowball smack in the middle of Jared's chest.

Jared was so shocked that his mouth was still formed in an O of surprise, his eyebrows drawing down in confusion, when Destiny joined in by tossing another one at him that just missed and went over his shoulder.

But when Gloria broke into a grin, it was as if some kind of spell had been broken. Like the high school football scrambler he had been, Jared suddenly ducked, dodged this way and that, then broke free of the little group, only to pop back up with a snowball of his own, which he lobbed gently at Gloria, who inadvertently missed getting caught with a direct hit because she had ducked her own head to form another snowball to throw at her husband.

Both Jared's snowball, meant for Gloria, and Gloria's own snowball scored direct hits on Ken Allerton's torso, momentarily erasing the grin that had begun to spread across his face when his wife threw the first volley.

In response to the unprovoked attack, Ken's brows drew together in mock outrage, and he bent down to collect a handful of snow as ammunition for himself.

At the same time, another snowball whizzed by Gloria's head—this time thrown by her own brother.

Jen just stood there, baffled and unable to believe what was happening, until she felt something cold and wet land on her own head, then break and slide slowly down her hair, with a tiny but very cold bit of it sliding into the warm space between her neck and her coat.

As she squirmed in discomfort, she turned around to see Destiny giving her a look somewhere between sheepish and victorious.

"You're okay, right?" Destiny said, with a worried look, when she saw Jen wasn't smiling. "I mean, I'm sorry if I—"

But before Destiny could finish, a snowball caught her on the arm, just as another landed on Jen, and another dropped to the barn floor between them.

They both whirled at the same time to discover that the three combatants on the other side of the aisle had now joined forces and teamed up on them.

As Jared and the Allertons let another round of snow missiles go, Destiny crouched to arm herself.

But Jen just threw back her head and laughed and laughed.

Twenty-Six

DESTINY STOOD IN FRONT of the full-length mirror in Beth's guest room and sighed. Jen had gussied the place up with a bottle of champagne and a vase of flowers to turn it into a suitable dressing room for the bridesmaids, but there was no amount of decoration that was going to help with the state of her bridesmaid's dress.

She'd thought, when the hem of the dress had first started to collect snow out in the barn, that she'd just be able to kick it off of the nap of the velvet, and it would be good as new. But it had taken them so long to clean out the barn that some of the snow on her skirt had melted, and some of it had turned to ice. And some of it, apparently, had gotten all the way up to her knees.

She'd managed to knock most of the snow and ice off before she came up the steps to the Dean house, and she'd quickly found a hand towel to dry the velvet off. But the traces of her adventures in the barn were unmistakable. The bodice and top of the skirt were made of even fields of lush velvet. But at the foot of the skirt, it turned into an unruly mess. If she had a velvet card for ironing the whole thing out again, and a couple of hours, she might have been able to make it look marginally presentable.

But as it stood, it almost looked as if the bottom of the dress was made from entirely different fabric from the rest. And as Destiny turned around in the mirror, it became clear that that fact was totally obvious from every angle—and probably even from a great distance.

Not to mention the fact that the dress, beautiful as it was, didn't make her feel beautiful. And it hadn't from the first time she'd tried it on. That morning, she'd gotten up, determined to fix whatever it was that hadn't looked right to her when she'd first finished it. But she'd checked everything from the fit over the hips to the dip of the neckline, and item by item, everything worked. Even the blue of the velvet was usually a flattering color on her.

But when she looked at herself in the mirror, she just hadn't felt right. And looking at herself now, she wondered if maybe that had always been the problem. Not that the bottom of the dress was ruined now, but that the dress had never really fit her, in the most fundamental ways, all along.

It wasn't so much that she'd sewn it wrong, or that the pattern had been bad, so that even an expert sewer couldn't have gotten a good dress out of it. It was that something about the dress didn't match *her*.

Standing in the mirror now, dressed up to the nines, she couldn't even tell anymore whether she looked good or bad, because all she felt was that she was pretending. Pretending to be somebody in a life she didn't have, somebody who had a place to wear a dress like that.

The only place she had to wear a dress like that, she told herself ruefully, was a barn. And she would have done a lot better in the barn that morning, she thought, twitching the still-damp, ruined hem of her dress, if she'd been wearing a pair of canvas overalls—or even her customary yoga pants. At least most of those were already stained, so that if anything else happened, nobody could tell what was new damage and what had already been there—including her.

On the opposite side of the door, out in the hall, someone knocked lightly.

Destiny had a sudden urge to try to do a quick change before whoever it was came in, and stuff the dress someplace nobody would ever find it. But she hadn't brought a change of clothes with her, or any kind of backup dress. That had been the whole plan of getting ready at home, when she'd come up with the idea: so much simpler not to have to haul the dress and curlers and makeup and all her other junk over with her to Beth's, then back again. She'd tucked a lipstick in her clutch purse and headed off happily, feeling like a model of country practicality.

But that meant that now, she didn't have any other options.

"It's me," Beth called from behind the door. "Can I come in?"

"Sure," Destiny said, opening the door.

As she did, she checked Beth's face, which was surrounded by a beautiful updo and a set of still-setting pin curls. Destiny had seen some kind of strain in Beth's expression the night before, although there hadn't been any time she could ask about it, between all the guests Beth had to greet and Destiny wrangling her own family. But having spent some time in the barn with Beth's future mother-in-law, Destiny had her guesses. And seeing the brittleness of Gloria's perfect facade, she had to wonder just how much else wasn't quite as perfect as it seemed in Beth's life.

As the two of them hugged each other, Destiny gave Beth an extra squeeze, her own kind of silent apology. She'd never thought anything hateful about Beth. But the jealousy she'd been feeling had reduced Beth to little more than a cardboard cutout in a charmed life. And standing with her now, in Beth's childhood home, where they'd spent so many hours together, she suddenly remembered again that Beth's life must be just as rich and strange—and complicated—as her own, in its own ways.

"How're you doing?" Destiny asked when they separated.

For the first time since Beth had been home, she gave Destiny what Destiny recognized as a real smile.

"Better," she said.

When Destiny gave her a questioning glance, she shook her head. "One day I'll tell you the whole story," she said. "But not this morning."

She took both Destiny's hands and spread them out so that she could see her dress.

"Oh, Destiny," she said. "You made this? It's so beautiful. And you're beautiful in it."

Sheepishly, Destiny flicked the hem of her dress, which should have resulted in a beautiful twirl of velvet, but instead wound up looking to her like a shudder that ran through the damp mess of the skirt's edge.

"It's seen better days," Destiny said. "I ran into some trouble out in the barn."

"What kind of trouble?" Beth demanded, her eyes widening in alarm.

"I'll tell you that someday," Destiny said with a smile. "But not today."

Beth grinned, then looked down to inspect the hem. She picked up the skirt and let it fan out.

"I see what you mean," she said. "But I don't think anybody else will notice."

"Really?" Destiny said. That seemed totally improbable to her. The disaster at the foot of her dress was by far the most noticeable thing in the world for her. But then again, maybe that's because it was what she was wearing. And maybe everybody else was paying more attention to their *own* outfits, just like she was to her own—and wouldn't have the time or attention to worry that much about hers.

Beth gave a decisive nod. "I think it's fine," she said. "And I'm the bride, so you have to do what I say."

"Yes, ma'am," Destiny said.

Beth glanced down at the hem again. "Actually," she said, "it looks pretty cool. My New Yorkers will probably think you paid extra for it."

Destiny laughed. "Watch out," she said. "Next year, everyone's dresses are going to look like this."

Beth gathered her in a hug. "Thanks for being part of this," she whispered in Destiny's ear. "I'm so glad you're here. That's all that matters to me."

"I wouldn't miss it for the world," Destiny said.

With a last squeeze, Beth released her.

"All right," she said, with a look at her watch. "I'm going to go have Mom take out these pin curls. And then I've got to put on the dress. Want to come down whenever you're ready?"

"You've got it," Destiny said.

With a smile, Beth slipped out of the room.

But just as Destiny turned back to check her own makeup, she knocked on the door again.

"Hey," Destiny said, turning around with mild concern, wondering what could possibly be bringing Beth back into the room.

But when the door opened, it was Carl's face she saw.

"Hey," she said, her concern growing. "Where are the kids?"

"Mrs. Fitzgerald has got them," Carl said. "Jen's got a whole little nursery set up in the living room. They're going to be making crafts during the ceremony."

He stepped into the room and shut the door behind him.

As he did, his eyes widened. "Honey," he said. "You look beautiful."

Destiny felt a little twinge of unease when he said this. She still wasn't at peace with the picture of herself she saw staring back at the mirror—or with the damage to her dress. And some part of the admiration she saw in Carl's eyes just made her wonder if he ever saw below her surface, to all the things that were really going on inside her. Should it be enough for her that he thought she was beautiful? she wondered. What did *she* think?

But even as these thoughts ran across her mind, something in the openness and love she saw in Carl's face made her soften. Her husband thought she was pretty. Maybe, she thought, it really was just that simple. And maybe it was a good thing.

She walked over to him and gave him a kiss as he wrapped his arms around her and ran his hands over the velvet of her dress, surprised by the unfamiliar softness.

"This is nice," he said, laughing. "You should wear velvet more often."

"It's very practical," Destiny said. "Wipe peanut butter on it, and it wipes right off."

Carl laughed and kissed her again. But then he pulled away and began to fumble in the pockets of his jacket.

"I have something for you," he said.

Destiny looked at him quizzically as he pulled what looked for all the world like a slightly greasy brown paper sack out of his pocket and tried to hide it quickly behind his back.

Then he cleared his throat. He clearly had something to say.

"I know this isn't exactly the heart of Manhattan," he said. "But I tried to get you something like *Breakfast at Tiffany's* this morning."

Then he held out the bag.

When Beth took it and unrolled the brown paper, there was a donut inside from the shop downtown.

And when she pulled it free of the paper, there was a beautiful diamond necklace draped clumsily across it.

Tears sprang to Destiny's eyes.

"You remembered," she half whispered.

"I actually got you that necklace last week," Carl said. "I wanted you to feel special for the wedding. It's just the donut I went out and got this morning."

He grinned, which Destiny interrupted with a long kiss.

"Wow," Carl said. "I should bring you jewelry every morning."

Destiny shook her head, still holding on to him. "It's not the jewelry," she said.

This time, Carl kissed her. "Donuts, then," he said.

Destiny pulled free of him, shook the sugar from the links of the gold chain, and handed it to Carl. "Will you put it on?"

She turned her back to him, and he laid the necklace around her throat and fastened it at the back of her neck. Then he kissed her cheek.

"And if it really matters that much to you to go eat a croissant in front of some store in New York," he said, "we can make that happen one day, too."

Destiny leaned back against him, letting her head nestle under his chin.

"But it isn't always so bad here, is it?" Carl asked.

"No," Destiny said, suddenly feeling like the luckiest woman in the world. "It isn't."

Twenty-Seven

STANDING IN THE BACK of the barn, surveying the results of their work, Gloria felt a pleasant feeling wash over her that it took her a moment to recognize as satisfaction.

Anyone who hadn't seen the piles of snow drifted up against the inside doors, or piled on the seats of the white chairs, which were now neatly arranged again in perfect rows, would have had trouble believing the story if they told them. The cement floor around the chairs, the aisle between them, and even the floor by the far door, which had been their dumping ground for the wheelbarrows full of the white stuff, was all blown and swept clean.

Jen, the wedding planner, had just turned on a small fleet of space heaters, which were quickly bringing the barn up to a temperature that made standing there in her thick down coat uncomfortable for Gloria—which was actually a good sign, because it meant it would be something close to comfortable by the time the guests began to stream in. And the young woman was busily doing one final sweep down the aisle with one of the old brooms she'd rooted out of the corner of the barn. But as far as Gloria could tell, it was unnecessary at this point—just one last once-over after the job was already done.

Gloria took a deep breath, and let it out in a satisfied sigh. It had been years since she'd done such hard work, and so fast, and she was surprised by how good it felt.

"Glory," Ken said behind her.

Gloria turned, not sure whether to be touched or alarmed that he was using his pet name for her. She felt like she'd barely heard him use that in years as well. And she wasn't sure what he meant by bringing it out now.

"I've got something for you," Ken said when she met his eyes. He grinned.

But Gloria's heart sank.

There had been something she liked about working side by side with him, knowing that she could trust him to move fast and make good decisions about how best to clear the barn for the wedding, and knowing that he didn't have any questions about whether he could trust her to do the same. That had never been a problem between them, that basic respect. And even though there had been so many other tensions between them, it had felt good to just live in that, even for a few moments.

But she'd heard exactly those same few words, *I've got something for you*, so many times before. At first, when they were young, it was a thrill. He'd given her things she'd never even dreamed of wanting: a pair of ruby earrings to replace the gold-plated hoops she'd planned to wear on their first date to a formal gathering with his parents. A necklace with a single diamond floating on an impossibly delicate gold chain, the diamond small and seemingly unassuming but, he told her, absolutely perfect in its structure and fire, worth far more than much larger gems.

They were even the words he'd used before he got down on one knee, so many years ago, to propose to her. With a ring from his family, but not one like the ones his mother now wore, with some of the clusters of jewels even bigger than her knuckles. This one had been his grandmother's ring, the only thing his grandfather could afford in the years before he made his fortune:

a scrap of diamond, set with chips of white topaz on either side. But even though he hadn't had much money, he'd already had an eye for the remarkable: the setting was silver, not even gold, but wrought by a jeweler who would one day become the darling of New York society, in part because Ken's grandfather kept returning to him even after he'd made his fortune.

These days, everyone who saw it on Gloria's hand thought the setting must be platinum, not silver. And Ken had actually offered to have it plated or even reset with more valuable metal or stones. But Gloria always refused. She never admitted it, because it seemed so sentimental to her, but the almost worthless ring was the most treasured piece of jewelry in her whole vast and ever-growing collection.

But since those early days, and those early gifts, Ken's announcements that he had something for her had started to ring more and more hollow. Now they came when he was returning from long trips, often after being out of any kind of real contact for days or weeks. At first, she'd missed him, wished for his return, hoped that next time he wouldn't be gone as long. But you could only hope those things for so long. And by now, it had been years since she let herself miss him when he was gone.

He hadn't stopped bringing her gifts when he returned. And some of them, even these days, hinted that he still remembered their earlier days together—a bit of turquoise from New Mexico, because he remembered her loving the vivid color when they first met, a scarf dyed sky blue because she'd always loved to throw her head back and look at the sky. But more and more, they felt to her like payment for a job—or a life—she would never have willingly signed up for. And even the things he remembered about their earlier days sometimes made her think about how many things he didn't seem to know about her now.

So when he said it to her now, she tried to smile, but her glance slid away from his.

"Oh?" she said.

Maybe she should have expected it, she told herself. After all, it was probably some kind of custom to give jewelry on the occasion of a wedding—at least in the Allerton family. But the thought of it just made her feel weary, bringing her back to the grind of her daily life after what had felt, for one lovely moment, like an escape from it.

Ken grinned. Then he stepped aside.

For a minute, Gloria couldn't figure out what in the world he was grinning about. Then her eyes adjusted to the dark, and she saw it. Nestled in the corner of the barn, an old-fashioned wooden sled.

"Remember?" Ken asked her.

Gloria's eyes lit up.

"Of course I do," she said.

It had been December when they first met, and just after their first date, a huge snowfall had blanketed the city. Ken had shown up the next afternoon with a sled that he'd bought in a local junk shop, and taken her to the nearest sledding hill in Central Park. It was there, at the end of their first ride down the slick slope, that they'd had their first kiss.

Gloria gazed down at the sled, thinking how far they'd come from that moment, the loveliness of the memory struggling with all the things that had calcified over it in the years since then.

But as she did, Ken picked it up and headed for the door.

"Wait," Gloria said, turning as he went. "Where are you going?"

"Sledding," Ken said. "Jen says there's a hill out here somewhere."

Gloria pushed back the thick suede of her jacket to reveal her watch.

"Ken," she said, hurrying after him into the bright light of the morning. "It's not even an hour till the wedding. We've got to get dressed."

"It doesn't take an hour to put on a dress," Ken called over his shoulder as she followed him out the door of the barn and began to trail after him around the corner.

"We need to get *ready*," Gloria amended.

"Glory," Ken said, turning back to her. "You always look beautiful."

Gloria drew up short, surprised.

By this time, they were standing on the top of a pretty significant rise. The barn was built on a slight hill over the surrounding fields, and on this side, the land also dipped down into a gully that extended the length of the rise and increased the slope by quite a lot, ending in a kind of bowl filled with snow. It wasn't exactly Pilgrim Hill in Central Park, but it promised a reasonable ride.

Gloria glanced around. They were so close to the time of the wedding that she wasn't just worried about getting ready in time. She was wondering if other guests might actually show up, fully dressed, while she and Ken were still wading around in the snow. But the coast was clear.

And when she looked back, Ken was seated on the sled, and was making exploratory feints with it, trying to gauge how slick the old runners would be on the snow. The sled was so old that traces of rust leaked into the bright white of the snowfall, but the runners showed every sign of serious speed. At one little tap from Ken, the sled leapt forward so quickly that he lurched off and had to make a grab for it and plant his feet firmly in the snow on either side to ensure it wouldn't be going anywhere else any time soon unless he wanted it to.

Ken looked up and patted the empty spot on the wooden seat, in between his legs. "Okay," he said. "Hop on."

"You're not serious," Gloria said. But as she looked at the long slope lying ahead of the sled, she felt a twinge of excitement, an echo of the feeling of adventure and hope she'd had as a young girl.

"Come on, Glory," Ken said, looking up at her. "What could go wrong?"

Immediately, Gloria's head filled with smart answers to that question. The list that began in her head could have taken all day for her to complete if she'd started rambling through it aloud. But something in the way Ken looked up at her stopped her.

The snow seemed to have done something to him, too. Maybe it was the invigorating power of the cold winter air. Or maybe it was just the light bouncing up off the snow from a hundred different directions. But he looked about twenty years younger. None of the lines had left his face, but somehow, the worry and the reserve had. He smiled up at her with a smile she hadn't seen in years—open and hopeful.

And she couldn't resist it.

An instant later, she had settled into the narrow wedge of the sled between his legs. For a moment, his arms encircled her, and she felt an unfamiliar wash of safety and warmth as she leaned back against him.

But before she could get used to that, he gave a mighty kick with his legs on each side of the sled, and suddenly they were hurtling down the hill together.

The old sled proved to have so much speed that Gloria's hair blew away from her face, and she went breathless with the thrill of the drop—and the sudden fear that they were going so fast they might actually zoom up the other side of the bowl of the little valley, and perhaps even take flight when they reached the lip of it.

She felt the dizzy sense that she was completely out of control. But as they barreled down the hill, she also had the unfamiliar sensation that she was, suddenly, perfectly free. It was exhilarating, and terrifying.

And it only lasted a moment.

At the bottom of the hill, the foot or so of snow that blanketed the rest of the countryside had piled up in a great drift. Without knowing the land, neither of them had been able to judge the difference. But when they got to the bottom of the bowl, the little sled, slick as it was, was suddenly mired in three feet of snow. And the impact knocked Ken and Gloria off the wooden slats, into the thick of it.

For a minute, Gloria just lay there, despite the fact that her hair was certainly full of flakes, looking up at the blue sky overhead, and drawing deep breaths of the cool air into her lungs, trying to keep the feeling of the ride with her.

But then Ken's face appeared above hers. And then blotted out the sky, leaning in for a lingering kiss.

When their lips parted, Ken tried to straighten up, his face suddenly embarrassed. But Gloria drew him down again for another.

When she released him this time, he stayed near, looking down into her eyes.

"You don't always have to go so soon," she said softly.

Ken's eyes searched hers. "It doesn't always feel like you want me around," he said.

Gloria took a deep breath. She reached for the inner door

that she'd gotten so good at closing against him, but somehow she couldn't find it in that instant. Instead, tears sprang into her eyes.

When he saw them, Ken's own eyes filled with concern. He reached up and clumsily tried to wipe away one of her tears with his gloved hand, smearing snowflakes all over her cheek.

Gloria smiled, blinking the tears away herself.

Then her eyes met his, and they simply looked at each other, for the first time in what might have been years.

It felt almost as if she were answering some other question when she told him, "I do."

Twenty-Eight

"CAN YOU BELIEVE THIS?" Beth whispered, looking out from the slit between the thick blue velvet curtains Jen had strung up in the back of the barn to make a makeshift dressing room for the bride, so that Beth could stay hidden from the guests as they gathered without having to tromp through the snow from her house in her wedding dress.

When she glanced at Jen beside her, she saw that Jen was looking out at the barn with an air of wonder that matched her own and actually went beyond her own. Jen seemed to be looking out at the gathering with something like actual disbelief, as if she wasn't just wondering at the weight of the moment, but couldn't quite believe it was actually happening.

Beth looked back out through the slit. The barn beyond was absolutely transformed from the shadowy, sun-dappled, dusty playground where she and Jen had spent so many hours dreaming and playing as girls. A ring of softly whirring heaters surrounded the guests, all seated in neat rows, with warmth. The arbor where Beth would stand with Tom in just a few short minutes was full of the flowers Beth and Jen had worked so hard to choose and order, but also lush with evergreens, a touch that Beth would never have thought of, but that brought tears of gratitude to her eyes, because they were a little touch of home in the midst of all the other strange new wonders. The air was full of the scents of pine and cinnamon, with the faintest trace of the handful of lilies in the arrangements that graced the aisle seats, creating a garden path for Beth to walk down whenever Jen gave the signal for the musicians to begin. And now all the seats were full, all the programs that had been waiting on the seats in the hands of her family and friends.

Beside Beth, Jen took a quick, deep breath and shook her head, as if trying to shake the last few cobwebs out of it.

"How are you doing?" Jen asked.

Beth took a deep breath of her own, giving herself a moment to really take it all in and answer the question. On the morning of her wedding, how was she doing? She could feel the fatigue in her mind, underneath all the excitement. She felt tears just under the surface of her mood—but happy ones, over all the faces of the friends and family who had been streaming into the barn now for the better part of the past hour. But most of all, she felt the leaping strength of hope, and the pull of love, drawing her forward toward the front of the crowd that had all come that day to celebrate her and Tom. And toward Tom.

"Good," Beth said. "I'm good. Thank you for this."

She squeezed Jen tightly, and for an instant, Jen squeezed back.

As they released each other, a gust of cold air blew into the makeshift room as Mitzi tromped in, followed closely by Beth's mother, both bundled in work coats, wearing snow boots, and clutching the skirts of their fancy dresses in their gloved hands.

"Here, here," Jen said, quickly relieving them of their coats, which she piled up on a table in the corner.

Beth's mother let a bag slide from her shoulder and pulled out a pair of strappy jeweled sandals and a smaller pair of silver pumps with sensible square heels.

"Those look comfortable," Jen said approvingly.

"You know what's comfortable?" Mitzi asked, pulling up the skirt of her silver dress to reveal the work boots she was still wearing. "These. And I don't see why I shouldn't keep them on. My skirt's so long no one will notice. And then I won't have to change again after the ceremony."

But as she said it, she was already grinning, kicking off the snowy boots, and reaching for the comfortable pumps.

"If you want to wear those boots, Grandma," Beth said with a mischievous grin, "it won't bother me."

Mitzi cocked an eyebrow at her granddaughter, well aware that her bluff had been called. "Oh, no," Mitzi said. "I wouldn't want to do anything to upset the bride."

Jen looked at Beth. "You're all set?" she asked.

Beth looked at her mother, then at her grandmother. There was so much love shining in each woman's eyes that it was hard for her to hold back her own tears of joy.

She looked back at Jen and nodded.

"As ready as I'll ever be," she said.

"All right," Jen said, giving her a quick peck on the cheek. "I'm going to go out and get us started."

She disappeared through the curtains as Beth's mother sat down on a nearby chair to fasten her shiny sandals around her ankles.

When her mother stood, Beth looked from her mother to her grandmother and back again, taking in the full sight of both of them done up to the nines in their silver dresses, their hair curled and coiffed, their lipstick perfect, at least for the moment.

"You two look wonderful," Beth said.

"Not one single person in that crowd is going to be looking at us," Mitzi said with a proud grin.

As she said it, the strains of Handel's Water Music began to drift through the curtain as the bridesmaids, who were hidden in a stall on the other side of the barn with the groomsmen, began to process down the aisle.

The sound of the music seemed to jolt something in Beth's mother's memory.

"Honey," she said, feeling in the voluminous folds of chiffon in her skirt, then turning back to rummage through the bag that had held their shoes. "I have something for you."

"It's all right," Beth said quickly, calculating how fast the music was running out. "We're about to—"

But before she could protest any further, her mother turned back and handed her a blue jay feather.

Immediately, the tears that Beth had been trying to hold back sprang into her eyes, in full force. She knew exactly what it was, before her mother even opened her mouth. When she'd been a girl, her father had brought her a jay feather from the yard one day, and she'd been so delighted with it that he'd never stopped. For years, any time he found one of the beautiful blue feathers with their black stripes and blue tips, he'd brought it in the house for her, even when she was a teenager and too stupid to be grateful for his constant gifts of love.

"Where did you find this?" Beth asked.

"I didn't find it," her mother said with a little shake of her head, probably partly meant to stop the tears that Beth could now see standing in her own mother's eyes. "Your dad did."

"He did?" Beth asked.

"Before he was too sick to move around," Mitzi broke in. "He went out and found it in the yard."

"He told me to keep it for you," Beth's mother said. "But I never could think of what the right moment would be. Until now."

She handed the feather to Beth, who lifted it to her cheek to feel the soft brush of the feather.

"I know he would have done anything in the world to be here for you today," her mother told her.

Beth threw her arms around her mother's neck. "He is," she said, her voice choked with tears. "He is."

Beyond the velvet curtains, the music changed to the Wedding March. They could hear the shuffle of over a hundred people as they all turned toward the aisle.

Quickly, Beth tucked the feather into the sky-blue ribbon that held together the stems of her bouquet of white lilies and snapdragons. Then she threaded one arm through her mother's arm, and the other through her grandmother's.

"Are you ready?" she asked.

Her grandmother grinned up at her, and her mother squeezed her hand.

Then all three of them stepped out through the curtain and came around the back of the gathering, to the center of the aisle.

The sight of the faces of almost everyone in the world who mattered most to her, all turned toward her at the same time, was like being knocked into by an actual wave of love: overwhelming, thrilling, and wonderful, all at the same time.

Behind her, Jen rushed to untangle the train of her dress, which was a simple boat neck that almost but not quite dropped off her shoulders into tiny cap sleeves, white silk covered with a white chiffon that made clean, beautiful lines as it fell in an A-line over her waist and hips, until it turned into a beautiful, lace-edged train around her feet.

With her mother on one side and her grandmother on the other, the three of them walked down the aisle as Beth took in smiles of joy and eyes bright with tears on the faces of her childhood friends, her closest colleagues, her high school history teacher, and Tom's buddies from the pool league. She knew exactly where Gloria and Ken would be seated: in the front row, on the right, and part of her didn't want to even look at them, but when she did, she almost didn't recognize them. Gloria's face was so full of joy that she looked almost like a bride herself. And beside her, Ken glowed with a happiness that Beth had never seen in him in all the years she'd known Tom.

Then, finally, Tom stepped forward from the line of groomsmen, which had been blocked from her vision until now by the faces of the crowd.

And as soon as she saw his face, she forgot everything else.

Twenty-Nine

SYLVIA GLANCED DOWN AT the hem of Destiny's dress as Destiny returned to their table, carrying a slice of wedding cake in each hand.

Around them, a few dozen other tables were scattered, set up in the barn after the audience chairs from the ceremony had been cleared and a dance floor had been laid out near what were apparently the back doors of the barn.

Overhead, the white paper globe lights that had lit the loft of the Dean barn the night before had been gathered into a giant bouquet, as if they were all pods of the same strange flower, and hoisted high in the air over the gathering, nestled in the peak of the barn between the rough old beams, a unique and beautiful temporary chandelier.

Now that dinner was over, many of the guests were milling around from table to table as the sun sank down in the sky, heading for one of Michigan's early afternoon sunsets. After all, Sylvia calculated, it was only a few days after the winter solstice, still one of the shortest days in the year—although she felt as if it was one of the longest she'd ever lived through herself.

Destiny laid a plate full of wedding cake in front of Sylvia and set a second at her own place, just beside her. Then she sank down into the seat next to Sylvia.

"Where'd you get your dress?" Sylvia asked.

Her own dress was from Bergdorf Goodman, bought after a Saturday whirlwind tour of Fifth Avenue–area shops that had also included Barneys and a handful of other fashion giants. In the end, she'd chosen a twenties-inspired dress, blue velvet, as Beth had asked, sleeveless, with a cowl neck that draped between two finger-thick straps, and a bias cut that skimmed her figure as if she were a 1930s screen siren. She loved the silk velvet and the way it slipped through her fingers, but she was fascinated by the effect the designer had gotten with Destiny's dress. It had a lovely mottled quality toward the hem, where the smooth fall of blue velvet was troubled by some process Sylvia had never seen. And obviously done by hand: the edges of the area that had been treated, whatever the treatment had been, were irregular, adding a special charm that wouldn't have been as lovely if the differ-ence in the fabric had begun at an industrial line. Instead, it almost gave the effect of an ombré, a darker color fading slowly into a lighter one. Except that it was all achieved, somehow, with a single tone of fabric.

Destiny looked at her warily, perhaps unwilling to give up her secret. "My dress?" she repeated. "I made it."

"You made it?" Sylvia asked in disbelief. She knew, in theory, that people made clothes. In fact, she sometimes joked that her tailors might actually know more about her than her therapist did. But she'd never encountered someone who'd made their own dress at a party like this before.

Quickly, though, she saw the advantage in it for her: she might be able to get her curiosity satisfied about the origins of the unique pattern of Destiny's skirt.

"Then did you do that work on the hem?"

Destiny glanced down at her skirt and looked back up, clearly confused by the question.

"The fabric," Sylvia clarified. "That—process." She reached out and plucked at the edge of Destiny's skirt, to show her what she was talking about: the part where the interesting texture began to appear in what was otherwise pretty run-of-the-mill velvet.

Destiny looked up at her with obvious shock that turned quickly to understanding. Then she pressed her lips together to suppress a smile—probably trying to hide her pride in the work out of Midwestern humility, Sylvia guessed.

"Oh," Destiny said. "That."

"You did it yourself?" Sylvia asked.

Destiny looked down at her dress again as Uncle Charlie walked up, also carrying multiple plates of wedding cake, and set one down in front of Nadine, who was seated just across from them at the same table, and one in front of Mitzi, who was seated beside her.

As he settled into his seat beside Nadine, Destiny looked up. "I guess you could say that," she said.

"So, what is it?" Sylvia asked, leaning in. "How did you do it?"

"Um," Destiny said, ducking her head again.

Maybe it was some kind of family secret, Sylvia thought. Passed down from grandmother to granddaughter, like a treasured recipe. She had a flash of worry that she might have overstepped by asking, but it was quickly overcome by her curiosity—and her desire to be the first in New York to bring the old custom back. If she could just find out what it was.

"It's—water," Destiny said finally, raising her head.

"Just . . ." Sylvia said, her mind racing. "Water?"

Destiny nodded.

Sylvia, catching the point, nodded along with her. A lot of the most beautiful textile processes, she had found, were much simpler than you'd think. "So," Sylvia said. "It's a water process?"

Destiny's eyes darted around the room, as if she was making sure the ghost of her grandmother wasn't around to haunt her for revealing the secret. Then she nodded.

"Okay," Sylvia said, leaning in farther and dropping her voice. "So if I asked them to do a"—she hesitated—"water process on this dress, when I get back to the city, they'll know what I mean?"

Destiny leaned back in her chair and regarded Sylvia for a minute, clearly calculating whether Sylvia could be trusted with the secret formula or not. Then she nodded.

"You should definitely ask them that," she said.

"Oh my goodness," Nadine said from the other side of the table.

"I'm telling you," Uncle Charlie said, his voice rising so they could clearly hear him. "I've never had anything so delicious."

"They don't serve cake in New York City?" Mitzi asked, with an arch of her eyebrow.

"Not like this," Uncle Charlie averred, gazing down at the cake as if it were a magnificent, glowing meteor that had just landed without fanfare on his plate. He took another bite and closed his eyes in bliss.

"It's our own strawberry jam they used," Nadine said quietly, as if she were giving up a state secret. "Between the layers."

"Strawberry!" Uncle Charlie exclaimed, as if this were a rare, exotic fruit whose name he'd only ever heard whispered before.

Nadine nodded.

"That girl of yours is fussy," Mitzi groused. "She said nothing the baker gave her tasted anything like the one we made."

"Well," Uncle Charlie said, "I can't disagree with her myself on that count. This tastes just like a summer day."

"You should taste the actual strawberries," Mitzi said. "Warm from the sun, fresh from the field. Nadine and I still pick them ourselves every year. And then we bring them home and set them up that night. The jam from the store's never that good, because they don't wait for the fruit to really get ripe."

"So that's the secret, eh?" Uncle Charlie asked.

Mitzi nodded, a hint of challenge in her eyes, as if she was daring him to disagree with her.

"And when do these strawberries arrive?" Uncle Charlie asked. "Do they appear from under the snow as soon as it melts off?"

Mitzi looked at him in exasperation, as if she couldn't decide whether he was actually as ignorant as he pretended to be about the ways of agriculture, or was just frivolous enough to be making a joke about something as important as Michigan strawberries, but in either case, she wasn't much impressed.

"First week of June," she said. "They come in in May, but they're never any good until they've had a chance to ripen for a week or two, so you don't have to hunt through half a dozen plants just to find a red one."

"You should come," Nadine said.

Sylvia didn't know Nadine well, but she knew that expression from a mile away. Beth's mother was doing her best to play it off as a light comment, but the intensity in her eyes gave her away. It was obvious, to Sylvia at least, that Nadine was struggling against how much she wanted to see him again. And when Sylvia's eyes met Destiny's, beside her, she could see the same interpretation in Destiny's eyes, by the mild rise of Destiny's eyebrows.

But Uncle Charlie had eyes only for Nadine. "You mean it?" he asked, his tone suddenly serious.

As Sylvia and Destiny tried to watch without staring, Nadine hesitated, thrown off by the sudden change in the tenor of the conversation. But then she nodded. "Well, sure," she said. "I mean, you're always welcome. . . ."

Uncle Charlie's face broke out into a grin. "There's just one problem I see with that," he said. Suddenly, Sylvia got a sense of the man he'd once been, but left behind: the life of any party. His charm, when he turned it on, had a powerful effect, even on her.

"And what's that?" Mitzi demanded, looking from Uncle Charlie to Nadine with her sharp eyes.

"I don't know if June will be soon enough," Uncle Charlie said.

A deep blush began to rise in Nadine's face. It was so unmistakable that it would have been by far the most remarkable thing about her expression—if it weren't for the power of her smile.

When Sylvia turned to share another glance with Destiny, Destiny had just turned away. Her husband, Carl, who had been over checking on the kids at the section where all of the little ones had been seated with a small troop of babysitters, had just come back. "Want to dance?" he asked her.

In answer, Destiny rose and put her hand in his, looking back over her shoulder to smile at Sylvia as she and Carl walked out onto the dance floor, where several couples were already swaying to the sounds of classic jazz standards played by a DJ.

Left alone on her side of the table, Sylvia glanced away from Nadine and Uncle Charlie, whose voices had now dropped to a level below what she could hear. She felt a little pang, as she always did, at being left alone. But she was used to it.

If the DJ had been playing something more danceable for one, she would have gotten to her feet to dance. Instead, she took a bite of the cake Destiny had brought her and discovered, to her surprise, that it actually was as delicious as Uncle Charlie insisted: a moist, dense yellow cake, layered with thick seams of strawberry jam, all topped with beautifully hand-piped cream cheese frosting.

But before she could take a second bite, she felt a hand on her shoulder.

And when she looked up, she saw Winston.

She barely recognized him. Yesterday, his idea of dressing up had been a slightly fancier quality of flannel. But today, he was dressed in a classic blue suit, a crisp white shirt, and a classy tie. He looked for all the world like the next James Bond. Until he grinned—and then he was all Winston again.

"Dance with me?" Winston asked.

"I'm sorry," Sylvia said, smiling to let him know she was joking. "Have we met?"

"I'm sure we have," Winston said. "But you're a little harder to recognize when you don't look like a drowned rat."

"Touché," Sylvia said, standing and slipping her hand into his.

For an instant after she did, she almost pulled it back again. It had seemed, for some reason, like the most natural thing in the world. But once she slid her fingers through his, she suddenly wondered whether he'd think the same thing, too.

Then his fingers tightened around hers, and she felt a rush of warmth and hope that she hadn't felt for a long time. And a sense of coming home that she wasn't sure she'd felt, ever.

The surprise of it struck her silent as he led her over to the dance floor. And when he wrapped his arms around her, she suddenly felt all the exhaustion of the trip and the past few days wash over her—and maybe a tiredness that went back far, far beyond that. It was all she could do not to curl up and fall asleep, like she had in his house.

But at the same time, as he took each step, leading her around the floor, he somehow gave her energy to take her own.

She took a deep breath, sighed, and looked into his eyes.

The intensity that she saw in the gaze looking back at her was so strong that she glanced away almost immediately.

Beside her, she caught a glimpse of Gloria and Ken Allerton. Gloria's head was thrown back with laughter, her normally perfectly coiffed blond bob an attractively tousled mess. Maybe it was the new style that seemed to have taken years off her age. Or maybe it was simply the smile. When she saw it, Sylvia suddenly realized that she'd never seen one so genuine on Gloria's face before. Gloria's smiles had always seemed like they might carry a threat at worst—or be some kind of mask, at best.

But now she simply looked happy. And it was so remarkable that Sylvia couldn't look away.

"They look like they're having a good time," Winston said, looking over.

"Yes," Sylvia said. "They do."

Thirty

"NOT BAD, MAN," BRADY said, seizing Tom's hand and then leaning forward to clap him on the back. "Not bad."

Beside him, Beth tried to smile. Brady had always driven her a little crazy, although he and Tom had been friends since before they could remember. But at least he was smiling, which she hadn't seen much of from him on the first day he arrived.

As Tom and Brady parted, Brady gave Beth a squeeze as well.

Then, as Tom looked down, his expression changed. "Did you really wear your Tessorinos out here through that snow?" he asked.

Beth suppressed a smile. Brady was famously fastidious about his clothes—especially his shoes, which were always from Italy, and always insanely expensive.

Brady shook his head and leaned in. "The old man I'm staying with, he made me take a pair of his boots," he said.

Now Beth did smile, because she could exactly picture how that conversation with Jen's dad must have gone.

"They were nice boots, too," Brady said. "He said he had them thirty years. I never saw anything worn in like that. And they fit me like a glove. You wouldn't believe it."

"You didn't . . ." Tom said, already guessing what had happened next.

Brady nodded. "At first he refused. Then I told him what I was willing to pay for a pair of shoes."

"I don't want to know," Tom said.

"I think I may have just financed a new tractor," Brady said with a wink. Then he clapped Tom on the shoulder. "Congratulations, man," he said. "Not bad. Not bad."

"Not bad?" Beth repeated under her breath as Brady wandered away into the crowd.

Tom slid his arm around her waist, squeezing her through the silk. "That's what he said when our parents took us to see the Parthenon in eighth grade," he said. "It's pretty much his highest compliment."

Beth laid her head on his shoulder, and suddenly wished she could just stay there forever as the exhaustion of the past few days washed over her.

"Hey," Tom said.

Brady had caught them in the corner of the barn, near where Tom and the groomsmen had waited before coming out for the ceremony. Now they were standing only a few feet from the little booth Jen had set up by stringing velvet curtains around an old pen. And for the first time that evening, perhaps because they'd now drifted to the edge of the crowd, when Brady walked away, no other guest rushed up to take his place.

Before anyone could see, Tom lifted the edge of the velvet curtain and drew Beth through.

That corner had always been a favorite of Beth's during the long afternoons she and Jen had spent in the barn. It was just small enough to feel cozy, and a great hiding place—not from each other, because both girls knew the barn too well, but from anyone who might come into the barn looking for them, because it was easy to duck down and be screened from sight if they didn't want to be found quite yet.

Beth hadn't seen it before the ceremony, but Jen had done a

beautiful job of fixing it up, with several chairs, a small table with a pitcher of water and some glasses, and even a two-seater settee that Jen had dug up from her basement, or thrifted at some shop.

When the velvet curtain fell back between them and their guests, Tom took Beth in his arms, looked down at her, then gave her a long kiss.

He'd kissed her a thousand times before, all kinds of different ways, kisses that were tender, or quick, or full of desire. But somehow, this one was different. It felt like it might go on forever—and it also carried the promise of forever with it.

Even as he was kissing her, her face broke into a smile.

"How are you doing?" he asked, looking down into her eyes.

Beth took a deep breath. "Good," she said.

Tom gave her another quick kiss. "That's what I like to hear," he said. Then his eyes turned mischievous. "So," he said. "Given the option, you'd do it again?"

Beth shook her head. "I'm not sure you were listening," she said. "I think the whole point is that we're *never* doing this again."

"Hm," Tom said, pretending to consider this. "Never eat cake again?"

Beth shook her head in exasperation. "We can eat cake," she said.

"Never kiss again?" Tom asked.

In answer, Beth kissed him.

"You're impossible," she said.

"Impossible to resist," Tom quipped.

As he gave her another squeeze, the velvet curtains twitched behind him. Beth looked over his shoulder, expecting to see Jen, who had been letting them know through the night where they needed to be next, and if there was anyone in particular they needed to talk with.

When she saw the face that appeared between the folds of velvet, though, her smile faded.

It was Gloria.

Quickly, Beth pasted another smile on her face, but Tom had already seen the flicker in her expression. And when he turned around, his own eyes were wary.

"Mom," he said, a note of warning in his tone.

As he did, Gloria pushed her way into the room—followed by Ken.

Beth tried to hold on to all the things she had told herself that morning, when she'd had so much clarity about the fact that this marriage was all about her and Tom, and it didn't matter what Gloria thought. Some part of her still believed that. But it was a lot harder to hold on to when Gloria was standing right there in front of her. And what did it mean that this time she had brought Ken along? Beth had already heard Gloria's arguments, and she'd had plenty of time to respond to them, even in her own mind, which was where it was most important. But she didn't know if she had it in her to stand up to the two of them, if Ken had come along this time to shore up his wife's demands. And Beth felt a twist in her heart at the thought of it. She had always gotten along so well with Ken. Did he really think that she was only after his son's money, too?

She could feel her stomach drop, and the hard knot that began to form inside of it. And she was so tired that she didn't know if she had any fight left in her.

Beside her, Tom tightened his grip around her waist. She knew he meant it to be comforting, but it had the opposite effect on her. She could feel him turning tense and worried, which were the last things she had ever wanted him to feel on the day he married her.

Gloria smiled, which was almost worse than if she'd narrowed her eyes. Beth didn't want to have to be the stubborn one, the one who seemed difficult, when everyone else was just smiling at one another and pretending everything was all right.

To Beth's relief, Tom was obviously trying to find a way to cut the interaction short, too. "Mom," he repeated, "we were just about to—"

"Just a minute," Gloria said, still smiling. "Just a minute. We have something we want to give to you."

Beth had to prevent herself from drawing back physically at that. She didn't know what she would do if Gloria waved that agreement under her nose one more time. And she didn't want to find out.

Gloria ducked her head and began to fumble with her bag.

"You know what," Beth began. "I really think that I—"

But before she could figure out exactly which excuse she wanted to offer, or finish her sentence, Gloria looked up, holding a small ring made of twisted wire.

"What's that?" Tom asked, his voice rising in surprise.

"It's your father's engagement ring," Gloria said, in a voice that sounded slightly giddy at the memory.

Tom glanced at his father inquiringly, but Ken just smiled.

"When he first asked me to marry him," Gloria said, "he had this beautiful ring, and I . . ." She glanced away, as if something about the memory still caused her faint pain. "I didn't have anything. But I wanted to give him something, too."

She looked back up and met Beth's eyes. "I had a paper clip," she said. "In my pocket. And so later that night, after he proposed, I told him he should have a ring, too, if he was going to give me one. I twisted this into a ring and gave it to him."

"I haven't seen that before," Tom said, peering down at the twisted metal.

"I don't think I've seen it since," Gloria said. "But I was just talking with your father, and he said—"

"I always carry it with me," Ken said. "I put it in the pocket of my billfold that night, and I never took it out."

Gloria looked between Tom and Beth, beaming, as if this was the best news she'd ever heard.

"So we thought . . ." she said, becoming a little flustered. "We wanted—I just—"

"We wanted to give this to you," Ken said, picking the ring up from Gloria's palm and handing it to Beth. "To welcome you to the family."

Beth looked down at the little circle of metal, her mind racing to keep up with whatever in the world was happening.

Gloria, who was watching her closely, caught her hesitation.

"I mean," she said, "I know it's nothing fancy. If you want, we could get it plated in gold. Or platinum," she added hurriedly. "Or even cast and remade completely from some better metal . . ." she tried, trailing off.

But Beth just shook her head, as her hand closed around the worthless, but precious, piece of metal.

"I like it just the way it is," she said.

Before she knew what was happening, Gloria had thrown her arms around her neck.

It took Beth a minute to realize that it was a genuine hug. But as soon as she did, she hugged Gloria back, and held on.

Thirty-One

"HONEY," JEN'S FATHER SAID, patting her on the back as he took up a post next to her near the front doors of the barn, where she was waiting for Winston, whom she'd sent over to the Dean barn to hitch up the horses to the ancient sleigh that was scheduled to take Beth and Tom off to their happily ever after—or at least to the warm SUV that was waiting down the road, just out of sight, to whisk them away to the airport at the end of the night. "You done good."

Jen smiled, slid her arm around his waist, and gave him a squeeze. "You have a good time, Dad?" she asked.

Her dad nodded vigorously.

But some mischievous glint in his eyes aroused her suspicions.

"Really," she said, her tone playful but still indicating her skepticism. "What was your favorite part?"

"When I sold my old boots to some young gentleman from the city for the price of a semester of your college," her dad said, his grin becoming triumphant.

"Dad," Jen said. "You didn't."

Her father gave an unrepentant nod. "I couldn't refuse," he said, trying his best to look as if he was the one who had been put upon. "He practically begged me." He shrugged and spread his hands in feigned innocence. "I didn't want to cause any problems at the wedding."

Jen shook her head.

"Well," her dad said, "I think this whole idea of starting a business in the barn might not be as bad as I thought. Only I'm thinking maybe it should be a shoe store. I'll collect old boots from everyone we know. All you have to do is get me a plane full of suckers from New York."

"Dad," Jen said. "You're terrible."

"I've got an old pair of waders out in the shed," her dad said. "You think he'd like them?"

"Don't you dare!" Jen exclaimed.

"I already told him about them," her dad said, grinning. "He's interested!"

"Well," Jen said. "If you're serious about a business in the barn, I guess we could arrange for a corner to serve as some kind of retail shop. . . ."

Her father barked with laughter. "Now who's the terrible one!" he exclaimed, and gave her a hug. "I'm proud of you, honey," he said when he let go. "This is beautiful."

"Thanks, Dad," Jen said.

For a second, the two of them stood side by side, looking back over the fairyland she had created out of the old working barn: the lights, the flowers, the swags of fabric and the glint of the glasses, and all the people still crowded inside, talking and laughing.

Then her father's eyes seemed to latch on to something in the crowd. And whatever it was he saw, they crinkled into another grin. But this one wasn't mischievous. It was full of warmth.

When Jen looked over, she saw why. Her dad had always liked Jared. So of course he was glad to see him coming up now—although Jen didn't know whether she should be glad or not herself. Or whether it mattered what she *should* feel, if that wasn't actually how she felt.

"Mr. Fitzgerald," Jared said, sticking his hand out.

"Jared," her dad said, giving it a hearty shake. "Good to see you, son."

"Likewise," Jared said with a grin.

"How's life treating you down in Texas?" her father asked.

"Oh, you know," Jared said. "I guess I like it. But I still miss . . ." He glanced at Jen, pausing as he searched for the word. "Michigan," he finally said.

"I expect you do," Jen's father said. "Well, if you'll excuse me, I've got to go see about a pair of boots."

"Oh," Jared said. "Well, good to see you."

Jen's father gave Jared's hand another hearty pump, then strode off into the crowd.

"Hey," Jared said. His eyes met Jen's, a question in them, but instead of holding her gaze, he glanced around. "This didn't turn out so bad, did it?" he asked.

Until this moment with her father, Jen hadn't really had the chance to stop and look around. The day had been so busy—and so crazy—that some part of her had hardly believed it was all real, even as it was happening.

Now that it was almost over, everything started to sink in: the beauty of the place, the sense of accomplishment—and her own bone-deep tiredness.

"It's hard to believe," Jen said. She turned to him. "Thank you," she said. "I couldn't have done it without you."

"Yeah," Jared said. "You could have. You'd have found a way."

Jen smiled. Some part of her knew he was right. "But since you were here, I didn't have to," she said.

Jared ducked his head, suddenly shy under the compliment. "Glad to do it," he said, looking at his shoes.

Inadvertently, Jen found herself sizing them up, wondering

what kind of price they'd fetch in her father's nascent store. But they weren't nearly banged up enough to be interesting to the burgeoning New York vintage agriculture market.

Suppressing a smile, Jen looked up.

"So," Jared said, glancing past her, into the gathering. "Where's Ed?"

Suddenly, Jared's skittishness made sense to Jen. He expected Ed to come up and join them at any moment. And it sure seemed like he wasn't looking forward to that.

"He didn't come tonight," Jen said.

Jared's eyebrows shot up. "He okay?" he asked.

Jen raised her eyebrows ruefully. "Yep," she said. "But when I talked to him earlier, he said it didn't seem like I'd probably have much time to spend with him tonight."

"So he didn't come?" Jared said. He was obviously trying to keep his tone light—and also obviously struggling with irritation at Ed, and elation of his own.

Jen gave her head a quick shake, and glanced out the crack in the barn door to see if Winston had arrived yet. Across the barn, she could see Beth and Tom slowly trying to make their way to the door, through a sea of well-wishes and goodbyes.

Jared, who had been standing beside her, looking out at the crowd, turned now so that they were face-to-face, and all he could see was her.

"Jen," he said. "I have no idea if you want to hear this from me. But I've got to say it. I've been missing you ever since . . ." He paused, as if the amount of time it had been came as news, even to him. "Ever since I left," he finished.

Jen took a breath and held it. For so long, she'd wanted to hear exactly those words. But did she still?

"I tried to tell myself it wasn't just you," Jared said. "That I was just homesick, or I needed to make friends, or . . ." He trailed off. "And that's all true," he said. "But seeing you this week . . ." He started to reach for her hand, then held himself back.

"It's you, Jen," he said. "It's always been you."

Jen stared back at him, a million emotions roiling through her mind and heart and whiting everything out, almost like the storm they'd both tramped through the night before.

"Do you think . . ." Jared said, then paused again, searching for words. "Do you think there's still any chance for us?"

As Jen stared back at him, the confusion in her mind only grew, until it seemed to be an actual sound, her thoughts and feelings sliding and grinding against one another.

Then she realized that what she was hearing was an actual sound—the tramp and snort of the pair of horses, and the hiss of metal on snow as Winston drove the sleigh right up to the barn door.

At the sight of it, she checked her watch. Good old Winston, who'd managed to be right where he was supposed to be, just like he promised, as always. And that meant that Beth and Tom needed to get in the sleigh now, to meet the SUV driver who had already texted he was waiting just down the road.

"I'm sorry," Jen said quickly to Jared. "I have to . . ."

She leaned into the door of the barn, and the giant old thing swung slowly open, revealing the sparkling white that still lay all around the barn, the twinkling lights of the giant tree between the two farms, and the fields that surrounded it, for miles, as well as the blue-black sky, now full of stars that sparkled like individual flakes of snow, suspended in the arch of the heavens above.

As she did, the faces of everyone in the barn turned toward the door, their attention caught by the change in the light, and the cool air now sweeping in.

Just as she'd hoped, that gave Beth and Tom the chance to make their excuses and head quickly for the door. Jen scooped up Tom's soft black coat and handed it to him as he came up, and after he shouldered into it, he wrapped a thick white fur around Beth.

But as the gathered guests crowded together in the door to see them off, Winston began to wave from the seat of the sleigh, pointing up at the sky.

Jen squinted into the dazzling array of stars, bright and clear, totally unobscured by the polluting light of any city streets.

Maybe it was the kind of thing they should point at and shout with joy over every night. But at first glance, it didn't look any different from any other beautiful night sky to her.

Then she saw it: a star that seemed to come loose, falling down the sky with a blazing tail, almost as if it were a flake of snow falling through the air to Earth.

Then another. And another.

The crowd burst into inarticulate sounds of wonder and surprise, then fell silent, until the next one appeared, when they they all *ooh*ed and *aah*ed as one again.

"Mommy!" Jen could hear Destiny's daughter, Jessie, saying somewhere in the crowd. "The stars can fly!"

Beth and Tom stood on the threshold of the barn, temporarily arrested by the show in the sky.

"A meteor shower," Beth said, glancing with a smile at Jen. "And perfectly timed. Did you arrange this, too?"

Jen shook her head. If there had been local notices about the night's phenomenon, she'd been too buried under the details of the wedding planning to notice it, let alone plan it into the night's festivities.

It was a pure gift, something she could never have planned or created in a million years—like love, and friendship, and family—a message of love and wonder from something far beyond any of them.

Beth gathered her in a hug. "Thanks for this," she whispered.

Then Beth and Tom were stepping out into the snow, as the meteors continued to blaze down the sky, and their guests broke out in a cheer. Then somebody began to sing: "Joy to the world . . ."

Another voice joined in, then another, until all the guests caught the tune together, singing it into the night and then beginning the verse again as Tom helped Beth up into the sleigh.

Drawing in a deep breath of the cold air, Jen felt a sense of completion, but also a pang of sadness that all the preparation and work of the past months and weeks had added up to this, and that, as beautiful as it was, it had already come and gone.

A tall form appeared beside her. Without even glancing over, she knew who it was: Jared. And just as it seemed she always had, she felt that same old urge to reach for him.

This time, she didn't resist it. Still watching as Beth settled into the curve of the sleigh back, and Tom curved his arm around her, Jen found Jared's hand, and slid her fingers between his.

For an instant, he started with surprise. And then his fingers closed around hers in a warm, strong grip.

Amidst cheers and calls of goodwill, the sleigh pulled away, into the night, as the meteors continued to pour down the sky.

And even though it was the end of the night, Jen suddenly felt a strange sense of hopefulness and a little frisson of excitement, as if something else was about to begin.

But in some strange way, it felt just like coming home.

CELESTE WINTERS was raised in snowy towns in Michigan, where she loved curling up by the fire with a good book at Christmas. She now lives and works in Brooklyn.